Amie L. Spurgeon

STRANGE EMOTIONS

AUSTIN MACAULEY
PUBLISHERS LTD.

A CIP catalogue record for this title is available from the British Library.

ISBN 9781786125484 (Paperback)
ISBN 9781786125491 (Hardback)
ISBN 9781786125507 (E-Book)

www.austinmacauley.com

First Published (2016)
Austin Macauley Publishers Ltd.
25 Canada Square
Canary Wharf
London
E14 5LQ

Chloe

Have you ever felt like you were alone in this world?

As I stared around my empty and lonely room, just looking out the window from my bed, my eyes were wide open looking out into the dark night. Outside felt so close to me, so loud, yet it was so far away. I had no thoughts, no feeling; like a body without a soul. I didn't know how long I was lying there; so calmly, not a flinch or a movement. My mind, for the first time, had rest without a thought. Finally, as I came round and started to move, it was morning. I knew I had to do something that day. Staying at home never did me any good. I would just linger round Jane.

I heard my aunt downstairs on the phone as usual. I had lived with my aunt for some time now, just me and her in a house that was suited for a bigger family. There once was a larger family living there; Jane and her husband, Uncle Lee, who sadly passed away four years ago, and my cousin Ben, who suddenly disappeared one morning. My aunt never spoke about him, wouldn't even mention his name and she would change the subject if you ever tried to talk about him. It was odd to me, as a mother and son bond was usually strong and I couldn't work out why he left. Ben was such a lovely cousin to me. When I used to visit them on the summer break, we always spent lots of time exploring the forest and the miles of wild land around us.

'Morning Aunt Jane,' I spoke calmly.

'Hey Chloe, did you have a nice sleep?'

I could tell Jane knew that I'd had many restless nights' sleeps; that she sometimes heard me walking around my room in the early hours in the morning.

'Yes I slept loads thank you, hey Aunt Jane has anyone called this morning? I thought I heard the phone ring but I wasn't sure,' I lied; I didn't think she would be happy if she knew I didn't sleep well, or at all most nights.

'Your friend Ella called, she wants you to call her back ASAP. She sounded ever so happy this morning Ella did.'

'Ok thank you, I will see you later,' I said in a hurry.

I got into my car and rummaged around my bag to find my mobile. It was making me stress thinking that I left it in my room. For some strange reason my temper was flaring up, I started taking deep breaths to steady my breathing. Sometimes that happened over nothing - *I blame my hormones*. I thought. I finally found my mobile and decided I should call Ella back.

'Hey Chloe,' Ella answered.

'Hey Ella, you called this morning, is everything ok? Jane said you sounded very happy this morning,' I said in a jolly voice, knowing that Ella was excited for some reason.

'I was wondering if you would like to go shopping down the mall as it's the summer sales,' said Ella very convincingly.

I thought how busy it was going to be on a Sunday during sales, 'Ok I'll come along. I have nothing planned this morning. I'm in my car now so I will come and get you. I won't be long, say ten.' I felt like my temper was showing in my tone.

As I made my way round the quiet road it relaxed me; I felt happier about seeing Ella. I had been working lots of long hours in the summer local campsite site, in the convenience store.

As I arrived in Ella's drive she was already there waiting for me; Ella was a very pretty girl. Her features were perfect in every way, with ocean blue eyes and clear skin, she was full of energy, so happy all the time it was almost like my energy was taken away, used up trying to keep up with the blonde bombshell. 'You took your time,' she smiled.

For some reason it was hard for me to crack a smile. My family thought I was odd but I never did smile much after my mother died and dad just went and left me to defend for myself; I was so young and helpless. It wasn't easy back then in England, and having to leave very little behind, smiling was the least of my worries.

'Ten minutes, like I said, I am not going to disappoint you today,' I chuckled. Ella started to blabber on. I was listening but it wasn't very interesting. I had no idea who she was talking about. Ella was in college studying fashion, she was very good at making her own clothes and making lots of friends. It was so easy for her as she was so friendly. I kind of figured out she was talking about a guy on the football team in the college she went to. I always knew Ella was going to do great things in life. I had never met a friend as good and kind as Ella. I met Ella one day when I was trying to find a present for Aunt Jane in a department store, she was working as a temp in the holidays.

We just arrived outside in the car park looking for a spot to park. It was so busy I never thought we would find a space. 'Chloe, Look! One over there! I'm so excited summer sales are awesome!' she said in a high-pitched voice, I wasn't excited, on the other hand. I wasn't into fashion; I was more an athletic and simple-style type.

'Hey El, do you think this will take time? Just I fancy a run later,' I didn't mean to sound rude.

'Shouldn't think so, I'm just mainly looking for inspiration; and a few new clothes of course!' said Ella. *Great, this means it is going to take all day,* I thought. As we finally got into the clothes department Ella's face lit up and the big smile on her face seemed even bigger.

As we walked around up and down an aisle full with lots of people brushing past, I started to feel tense. My muscles were stiffening and my chest felt tighter; I could feel my hands shaking. All of a sudden I dashed out the shop. The aisles felt as if they were stretching out in my vision, feeling a lot further away than they should.

I was calming myself down from the frustration of people being inconsiderate and not moving.

'Chloe,' Ella shouted out.

I felt awful running out on her but I had to, it's not like I wanted to, it was just that I felt really strange. All of a sudden Ella ran out behind me with two bags full of new items she had invested in 'Chloe are you ok? What happened? One minute you were there and the next you had gone so fast,' said Ella curiously.

'I'm sorry, can we just go please?' I said with my breath still fast.

As I got back into my little black car Ella looked at me in a way she had never done before, as if she was looking at a stranger.

'Chloe I think you need to see someone, get some tests done, you don't look so well. It's like someone has drawn dark circles around your eyes and you're so tensed up,' Ella said seriously. Her smile was gone and she was frowning.

'I'm fine just a bit tired, just feeling hungry actually,' there was a long silence in my car, it made me on edge. We weren't far from Ella's home. She lived closer to town than the countryside. As I parked on Ella's drive I thought I had better break the ice.

'El I am fine, honestly, and thank you for your concern. I'll give you a call after work tomorrow,' I said peaceably.

'Ok Chloe, but consider what I said and we will speak tomorrow,' Ella said.

As I was driving home I started to wonder *was I really ill?* I felt healthy and strong. I did think that it was unusual for someone who hardly sleeps to stay awake for so long without feeling weak, but my body was in great shape: I could run for hours and still feel energised. When I ran I loved the feeling of the air running through my long, dark brown hair, brushing off my face: the feeling of being free and wild. The peace was so calming, just hearing the breeze through the trees and the smell of nature around me.

As I got back to the house and walked through the front door Aunt Jane was sat drawing. I had never seen any of Jane's pictures, but I was sure they were amazing. Jane never looked up as I walked in, 'I'm going for a run in the forest I will be back soon ready to eat, ok?' I said in a hurry.

'Ok Chloe, I will cook you up your favourite, be careful won't you now?' Aunt Jane said.

She seemed so laid back. As I went upstairs to change into my shorts and t-shirt I looked outside; it was very cloudy and looked like it was cold, but I didn't really feel the cold that often so it wouldn't affect me.

I got to the edge of the forest and parked up in a slip way, I felt so excited to get started. I warmed up with a walk, and then I was running with the air through my hair, and the freedom, on my own. The frustration of my outburst in the mall was gone and my head felt clear.

It was starting to get dark as I took a rest before heading back. Something wasn't feeling right, I felt like I was being watched from a distance. I was starting to get scared, looking around quickly. Then I noticed a slight movement from the trees. It had seemed so still that I couldn't hear a thing at all. No one lived near there, I'd never seen or heard people in the forest in the past, where I ran. I heard a twig snap in the distance! That was it. My heart was racing and I ran so fast it was like I couldn't see in front of me. I couldn't look behind either. I found my car and, rushing to get in, I couldn't get my keys in quick enough to get the engine starting. My heart was racing!

On my way home I began driving as fast as possible, feeling that my body was stiff and my muscles were locked in place. My whole body shaking, my eyes wide open trying to stay alert, saying in my mind, *what just happened?*

I finally got back to the house; Aunt Jane was still up waiting for me.

'Oh dear, what happened honey? Dinner is in the microwave and I really think you will like it,' Jane said in a very relaxed way. I thought she would at least ask to see why I was so distressed.

'There was something in the forest, I couldn't tell what in the distance.' Jane never replied. I guessed she was still drawing and wished not to be disturbed.

I sat down to fill my empty stomach, food had never tasted so good as at that moment. My taste buds went wild, especially with the tender taste of the meat. Aunt Jane fed me loads of meat, it was with every meal. Today she cooked me steak and chips with salad, it was the best. Jane loved to cook – she was very good at it too. I wouldn't have known how to.

'Night Jane I'm off to bed,' I said. I was still shaken up from the forest experience. I couldn't work out whether it was an animal or if it really was someone watching in the distance.

I lay in my bed, looking up above me, feeling pretty empty and wishing my mum was still alive to comfort me.

I know I'm getting a bit old for a hug at eighteen. Maybe that's why Aunt Jane doesn't comfort me! I thought.

My mum was just like me, with long, thick, dark, wavy hair and warm hazel eyes with fair, clear skin. It all seemed like a distant memory back in England even though it was 9 years ago since I moved.

I didn't miss England much. I enjoyed my summer break here in the US, with my cousin, Ben, and with Jane. I had so much fun; we even went fishing down at the lake. I wasn't very good at fishing but Ben was extremely good, it was his hobby, he also enjoyed running, he was faster than me. Guess it's because he was three years older. Those were good times and I miss Ben. I couldn't believe he left not that long before my arrival. I wish I knew where he went, just so I could tell him I miss him, and Aunt Jane isn't the same without him.

I started to drift off asleep, I felt like all the worry and shock just drained away.

With my eyes closed, the peace felt great after my hectic day, but I was back there dreaming of running in the forest.

Ben was right next to me, we were laughing at each other and then I looked back and he was gone. I was scared of being alone as it was getting late, the moon was out and the clouds were dark. I heard howling in the background and I saw what looked like a man in a black hooded jacket, with the hood up so I couldn't see his face. I started running as fast as I could; he was right behind me, keeping up. I was trying to focus on where I was running. I could hear his feet thud in long strides. It got dark so quickly, and it started to rain heavily making it hard to run with the dirt being slippery. I fell quickly to the ground as I slipped on the wet dirt, there was no one to be seen, then all of a sudden, out of nowhere, Ben reached over to grab my hand. I wasn't sure if it was him, it was so dark, but the shock of Ben's sudden appearance woke me up out of this nightmare with clammy palms. I hoped I would never dream again.

Changes

It was finally early morning and the sun was rising. I was still shaking from my nightmare last night. I got up out of bed and went to the bathroom to wash my face, as I ran the tap and poured warm water on my pale face, I looked up in horror when I saw my reflection in the mirror. I looked different, my hair was darker and slightly longer, my eyes were bright, pure green - not hazel anymore. The shadow under my eyes seem darker, more noticeable. My eyelashes were thicker and long. I put my hands on my face, it felt soft like silk, and I would never have thought I'd see my face paler. *What is going on?* I thought in my head, *this is unreal; how could I have such a drastic change overnight?* I kept looking in the mirror closing my eyes and opening them again hoping I was still asleep. My heart was racing again and my palms still clammy. Things started to get bleary.

'Oh no, this is wrong! How can I go anywhere looking like this?' I said out loud. *What will Aunt Jane say, how will Ella react to this?* I couldn't look in the mirror any longer, I closed my eyes tight, trying one last time to wake up still thinking *this could all be a bad dream.* As my eyes opened I still looked the same, *it's crazy.* Last night I was the same old Chloe and now I had stunning, bright green eyes, but sadly the darkness under them and the paleness of my skin were worse! I had to think quickly as I knew I would bump into Jane soon. I knew this wasn't my fault but I didn't want to freak anyone out either.

Quickly, I ran into my room and put my hair back in a bun to hide the fast growth of my hair. I was searching in my drawers for make-up, *I never wear make-up normally but I guess it will look better than a zombie*, I joked. *Great I've found it;* I looked back in the mirror to find a way to brighten my face. I used a light concealer under my eyes to brighten the darkness, I saw that I had some foundation a bit darker than usual, for my skin, hopefully this would work. 'Ah, maybe a bit of mascara to make the green look darker. Nope that simply won't do.'

I manage to calm down the difference in my face, ready to face the day. I wanted to be looking how I did yesterday; I wasn't quite sure if it was better or not. 'Morning Aunt Jane,' I said as I was heading down the stairs.

'You're up early Chloe, was it another nightmare?' Jane said casually.

'How did you know I had a nightmare?' I said, unaware that she was awake when I'd been dreaming.

'Chloe, I heard you screaming honey. It didn't sound pleasant,' Jane said worriedly. *Oh gosh I hope I didn't say Ben's name out loud,* I thought.

'Oh right, well I'm fine it was nothing,' I said grumpily. As I went downstairs, I went to the kitchen to make some breakfast before I went to work. I wasn't sure if I should go to the campsite as I was starting to feel unwell like I was going to be sick. I felt hotter than usual, it was disturbing knowing that I was going through these strange changes. Some advice needed to be given. *Maybe I should go to the doctors like Ella said.* I sat down at the small table in the kitchen eating a large bowl of cereal. As I was satisfying my hunger, I was still thinking about an explanation for my eyes, I could understand that my hair could have a freak growth spurt and my skin look paler from feeling ill. But how could my eyes change so beautifully? The bright, outstanding green; and it looked like I was wearing eye liner. My lashes looked longer and fuller, almost false. I wanted to stare at the mirror again as I was so fascinated. I'd finally decided I wasn't going to work today; it was too risky, people asking questions which I would not have any answers for. *It might be best to have some time off to sort out this unknown illness I must have. I think I may have to see someone today.*

As I was cleaning up what I had used for breakfast, I thought to myself, *could I have the illness that my mum died from*? As I was so uncertain, and worrying what could be wrong with me, I decided I would have to see Doctor Harvey. So I snuck back upstairs to my room to call for an appointment; keeping it a secret from Aunt Jane seemed like the right thing to do. I didn't like secrets very much as I knew there were so many secrets from me. Sometimes it was for the best, to keep these secrets, but I always wondered if it was a burden in their minds. As I took my mobile out of my bag I couldn't help but think phoning the doctor might be the wrong thing to do. How would they react if I started to tell them it happened all in one night? They might think I was crazy and put me on pills. But it was a risk I was willing to take for the truth of these bizarre unreal differences.

'Hello my name is Chloe Day and I need an urgent appointment please!' I said, knowing it may be short notice to be seen at my local practice. But I was desperate, with my shaky fingers crossed, hoping.

'Yes Miss Day but I'm afraid nothing is available,' the reception lady said to me as if she didn't give a damn.

'Please it's very important I see my doctor today. I wouldn't be calling if I didn't need to see my doctor ASAP,' I said raising my voice slightly.

'Ok Miss Day if you can make it here in twenty minutes then I can fit you in. But if you're late then I'm afraid you will not be seen today,' said the receptionist.

'Fine, I will be there, and I won't be late,' this time my voice was raised and my temper gave me a pain in my chest.

As I ran down the stairs without saying goodbye to Jane I got into my car and made my way. I managed to walk into the practice on time. I falsely glanced at the lady I spoke to. 'Chloe Day,' I said

'If you'd like to take a seat, Doctor Harvey will see to you shortly,' said the receptionist. Huh, well now I started to think, *then why all the rushing about?* I sat down in the waiting area that looked so clean you could eat off the floor. The practice wasn't very large; it was a cosy room, with magazines and a coffee dispenser. Looking around at all the sick people today, I was feeling a bit guilty, but I knew that I was meant to be there as much as them, even if I did look slightly healthy. A few minutes went by, then I realised a car was outside near mine, with a dark haired guy with sun glasses on inside. He was just staring straight through the window in my direction. I didn't know who he was looking for but I had a bad feeling in my guts about this guy. 'Miss Day,' my name was called from reception; 'Doctor Harvey is ready now, sorry for the wait,' said the receptionist apologetically. I took one last look out the window to see if the stranger was still there, sadly he was still in his big truck looking down at a book of some sort. I looked away and headed down the corridor to Dr Harvey's private room.

'Hello Chloe, how can I help you? Take a seat please if you wish,' said the doctor in his very professional voice. Doctor Harvey had been taking care of me and Jane. He'd been Aunt Jane's consultant for years.

'Thank you for seeing me today,' I said with a frog in my throat, 'I've not been myself lately, I've been experiencing a lot of pains in my chest, changes in breathing, I also get the shakes when I'm frustrated. For some reason I hardly sleep at night. But I'm never tired if I don't,' I said in pain, not wanting these words to fall out of my mouth.

'Chloe it sounds a bit like anxiety, I think we will take a blood sample in the mean time to find any abnormalities,' said the doctor, relaxed.

I've never had a blood test done before, I can't actually remember the last time I had an injection. As Doctor Harvey was setting up for the test, I sat myself on the examining bed. I decided I wasn't going to watch and looked away, otherwise I could pass out. 'Ok Chloe it won't hurt you will just feel a slight sting,' said Doctor Harvey. I took a deep breath, trying to control my consistent shaking as I looked to the opposite side.

'Ok I'm ready,' I said, trying to control this frog in my throat. I couldn't feel anything, not even a sting, the doctor stopped and stepped away from me. He took a long hard look at me as if he was in shock. I looked down at my arm. There wasn't a mark on me, not even a sign of bleeding! I knew something was wrong and was just waiting for Doctor Harvey to talk again.

'How did you do that?' he said in horror.

'I didn't do anything! I don't know what you think I have done?' I said, almost shouting.

'Chloe how did you stop the needle piercing your skin? You must tell me!' said Doctor Harvey raising his voice, about to lose his patience.

I couldn't move or talk or explain the impossible. How was it possible? How could I repel against a sharp object, stop it from piercing my fragile skin?

'You have to believe me sir I don't know how this happened! What if we try again? It may work,' I said, trying to think positively.

'I'm afraid not, as you have just broken this needle and I have many patients to see today, I think you should leave?' he said as if he was scared of me, his voice was trembling.

Doctor Harvey turned his back the other way. He was so horrified by me that I thought I'd better leave before this got out of hand. I was not sure which shocked me more, whether it was the test failure or the doctor rejecting me.

I walked to my car and felt my knees go weak with my head feeling light. I stopped immediately when I realised the guy in the truck was still there. Taking a deep breath, brushing my hair off my shoulders, I took a step forward; all of a sudden this distinctive scent came to my nose. The scent was so beautiful, so addictive like flowers in spring. I wondered at why it was so sudden, and how intoxicating the scent felt. Looking around the car park, my eyes caught sight of the guy in the truck. Then all of a sudden he looked up without his glasses on; he had a perfect sculpted face with the most amazing blue eyes which you could have noticed a mile away. I'd never felt so drawn to a male like this before, he had dark short hair with tanned skin, almost Mediterranean, and short facial stubble.

We must have been looking at each other for a long time, not even realising how awkward this was. But looking away from this amazingly stunning guy who caught my eye wasn't an option. I had completely forgotten for that moment what happened with Doctor Harvey, I felt a strong chemistry towards him. *I don't even know who he is and why he is here looking at me.* I wondered if he was feeling what I felt, I wondered if it was destiny to meet me here of all places. His face dropped, looking angry, like he had seen something disagreeable. The handsome man started the engine and the wheels spun away, his truck going at some speed towards the main road. I could still smell the scent lingering in my sinuses. I finally got into my car and the memory of my experience was haunting me; all of the strange happenings just didn't add up.

Driving back out of town, I could feel my body shaking, wanting something. I really was getting confused about what was going on with my body, my mind, and soul. If this was all part of getting older I was not in for an easy life that's for sure. *No one knows who I am, not really. I don't even know who I am yet. Where I'm heading to in life itself.* I couldn't even concentrate on the road but somehow I made it home safe.

I dumped my car on the drive and ran into the house feeling pretty mad and upset. *I want to know these secrets and I demand them now, I can't explain how emotional I feel right now but this has got to end someway.* I'd walked into the dark sitting room shouting for Jane, 'Aunt Jane! Jane,' I said with anger.

I didn't even consider why I was about to have it out with Jane but it seemed like a good idea. Jane came down the stairs with a sour face, looking like she was going to put me back in my place. But not even her expression could stop me freaking out right then.

'Chloe what is wrong with you? Can you lower your voice please?' Aunt Jane said very seriously.

'I want to know how my mum died. Why did Ben leave? And also, why am I so different to everybody else?' I said, my voice trembling and tears in my new beautiful eyes.

'Chloe I will talk to you once you have calmed down, I suggest you sleep it off and I will talk to you after work tomorrow,' Jane said in a forceful tone of voice.

I hurried into the kitchen and grabbed some snacks. I was so hungry as I'd been out a large part of the day. Then I ran upstairs away from Aunt Jane, I heard her cry for the first time. *I'm in such a mess and confused, I don't know how I can get out of this.*

I felt really sorry for myself and Jane, I wanted to apologise right away. But time in my room by myself couldn't be worse than my day so far. It was early evening before I calmed down, looking in my mirror wiping the make-up away from my face. *This has to be the worst day so far since my mum died,* even though I saw the most beautiful guy I've ever seen in my whole entire life. I was pleased to know that tomorrow I would talk properly to Aunt Jane about my situation, even if it was going to be hard digging up the past. My heart knew it was in the right place, but my mind didn't.

I could feel my soul wasting away the more I thought about the past and present, and how I may never know what had occurred. I was scared of sleeping after my nightmare last night. I was thinking that I didn't want to be more scared than I already was.

As it got dark outside I turned off the light and closed the curtains. Lying on my bed in my small bedroom, I flicked the lamp on which was on my bed side cabinet. I felt more comfort, not being in the dark. I looked at the picture beside my bed of my parents, thinking how much I needed their support and how I missed them dearly.

Drifting off to sleep after an hour of gazing at the photo, I felt so peaceful and blissful. After managing to sleep for four hours I woke up feeling refreshed. I looked at my clock and realised it was only one in the morning. I stayed in bed thinking about the amazing dream I'd had. Ever since I laid eyes on the mystery guy that day, whenever I had a clear thought from my misery he was in my head. I felt even warmer, and I was smiling and for the first time I meant to. I could still smell his scent that felt addictive to me, his eyes, his dark hair, his face so perfect like it was sculpted by an angel. This was insanity, crazy! Feeling this way about a complete stranger I'd never seen before in my life. I didn't feel like dropping my image of this hunk out of my mind yet, it would only lead to pain from my fall out from yesterday. He would keep me distracted for hours and hours; time seemed priceless when I wanted to keep him in my mind. I started to hear the birds singing as morning dawned. I lay there just waiting for my alarm to bleep. Then I got up and headed into the shower to be ready for work, trying not to wake Jane up. I left my make-up bag under the sink for my new daily routine. I still had reason to believe I needed to put a mask on my face.

Secrets

'Aunty Jane!' I called out to try and patch things up. 'Aunt Jane are you awake? It's 7 o'clock,' *Hmm how odd; no answer.*

It was very weird Jane wasn't downstairs before me, I wondered if she was still upset from last night's argument. It occurred to me to leave a note downstairs. I decided to leave the note just before I left, as I was downstairs finishing up my large bowl of cereal. Looking out of the window at my car as I ate, I heard a loud engine noise coming up the road. Not many people used this road as there were not many houses nearby, it just led to the forest. I couldn't believe my eyes when I saw the truck with the beautiful mystery guy driving. He slowed down by my drive where my car was parked; I couldn't see his stunning face carved by angels. He stopped for a split few seconds and drove on.

I finally started breathing, I had butterflies in my stomach. I started to like the sensation I got when I saw and thought of him. I felt the urge to follow him in my car. I'd started to write the letter for Jane, as there was no sign of Jane coming downstairs to face me any time soon.

To Jane

I've left you a note as I'm going to work today. I am ever so sorry for my attitude yesterday evening, and I hope we can still talk tonight. Don't worry about dinner as I am going to ask Ella out to the steak diner with me. Hope you have a lovely day and don't do too much.

Lots and lots of love Chloe xxx.

I got in my car on my way to work singing along to the stereo, I wondered if anyone would see behind my mask, and notice what had occurred. After my little outburst yesterday I had my anger and temper under control. I couldn't help but wonder why Doctor Harvey never did more examinations on me to give me a solution for my dilemma. I had just arrived at the campsite, as I pulled up to the hut I noticed a new member of staff. *Oh no,* I hoped they hadn't replaced me because I didn't turn up yesterday. I didn't see any camp managers around the site, it was still fairly quiet as campers were still in their tents or camper vans.

'Hello my name's Tim, can I help you?' said the new team member.

Tim was very tall and in good physique. Tim had long, jet black, scruffy hair over his dark skinned face. He was also dressed very averagely and looked like he'd been wearing his clothes from ten years ago. It struck me that he wasn't from around here.

'Hello I'm Chloe I work here,' I said slightly sarcastically.

'Oh sorry,' he said, apologetic, 'they did tell me I would be working with you today. I must have forgot, sorry,' he tilted his face down to look at the floor. I thought he was shy for someone the same age as me, I guessed.

'Accepted,' I grinned. 'Tell me about yourself as we've got time, I haven't seen you around before. Sorry, if I sound nosey do tell me to stop,' I said, hoping for it to not be boring, at least to be more interesting than the stories of the other temps that come and go.

'I move from camp to camp where there is work, there isn't much to tell. I do like your accent, very British,' he smiled at me, finally taking his eyes off the floor.

'What about your family where are they? Don't they mind you travelling,' I said, more interested.

'I don't have family, but you weren't to know. As soon as I was old enough to leave and care for myself, I left to be free and on my own,' he said, surprisingly fine about the subject. That may have made some sense of his appearance, he was shy, on his own, and in shape, ok I understood now.

We were talking all morning about growing up and moving on from our troubled pasts. Tim was a fantastic character, making me laugh at the least funny of conversations. As the day went on I got in contact with Ella to go for dinner. I thought about inviting Tim along to dinner with me and Ella as I thought that Ella and Tim would hit it off. I decided that maybe I should spend more time with the blonde bombshell on my own.

I was not feeling too good by late afternoon; I felt my teeth in pain, almost as if they were stretching my gums.

I was thinking about how I was going to start the conversation with Aunt Jane. If I could just wake up tomorrow with the explanation for our strange family secrets, then I might feel better.

'Chloe I have to leave now; I will see you tomorrow won't I?' said Tim as if he was in a rush to go. *We still have an hour 'til we close,* I thought to myself.

'Yeah, I'm working tomorrow. I will see you–' before I got to finish my sentence, Tim was gone.

It was weird how he was in a rush, Tim never spoke about knowing anyone, nor did he say he had to be somewhere that night. As I was shutting up the shop, I noticed a big shadow on the edge of camp in the forest. I couldn't work out what it was, whether it was a bear or a lost dog, but it was too big. The camp site wasn't very big: there was just the shop and public wash huts. The camp was surrounded by great huge trees that were compacted close together, making the forest darker. The camp was more for adults as it would not appeal to families with children.

I got into my car to meet Ella and looked back; the shadow was nowhere to be seen. I looked in my mirror to top up my makeup. I couldn't believe once again what I was seeing; my eyes were back, the green was bright round the edges, my teeth seemed whiter, and the dark shadow under my eyes was disappearing. I wished I could only know what was happening to me, then I just might have been able to accept this.

I took a deep breath and headed out of the camp exit, it was only a twenty-minute drive to Ella's house from camp. I was excited to see Ella, but at the same time I was scared, *I just hope Ella doesn't say anything about my new appearance.* The road was normally quiet with no other drivers in sight. I passed my parking spot for when I went running, it gave me a shiver; I thought to myself that I needed to go back sooner or later. I noticed a truck driving the opposite way in the distance and I thought to myself, *I've seen that same truck before.* It was him, that guy who I dreamed about, who seemed to be at every turn. As the hunky guy went past we made eye contact at one stage, my heart felt like it ached, I felt like I was floating; looking into his dark mysterious eyes I felt warm. I thought that I should follow him and introduce myself, but then he might have thought I was weird! I couldn't help but think he was driving around to find me. No, it was ridiculous to think that.

The camp and forest were the only places along the road. *Oh my, why didn't I think of this before? Maybe he was in the forest that time. What if he was stalking me and watching my every move? What if I should be scared of this man?* I was worried now at my thoughts, I did not want to be scared of him I just wanted to fall for this young man. As I got to Ella's house, I looked at how sweet it was. Ella's home wasn't very big, even though there were four of her family under that small roof. Ella's parents were very wealthy, but they believed in keeping an average life. As I walked into the small porch, Ella's mum was already ready to greet me.

'Hello Chloe, how are you?' said Ella's mum, speaking pleasantly.

'I'm very well thank you,' I said as if I was well, I didn't want to say much to draw too much attention to myself.

'Now Chloe, just to warn you, Ella isn't in the greatest of moods today, she's had some bad news,' she said with the most serious expression on her face. 'I'm hoping you can cheer her up for me.'

Ella came down the wooden stairs in the hallway, it broke the conversation. 'Hi,' Ella said, looking unbelievably miserable.

I knew something was up with her. As she walked straight past me out the front door, I followed behind her. We got in my car and the silence was a killer.

'So Ella, you hungry?' I said, trying to start a conversation. She didn't answer, 'You ok? You seem very quiet,' I said, determined to get some words from Ella.

'Look I'm fine ok, stop asking questions! It's none of your business Chloe, why should I even talk to you, have you looked at yourself recently?' she said in a tone which I never thought I would hear from her.

'I'm worried that's all, am I not allowed to be concerned?' at this point I was driving, I didn't want this conversation now.

'You don't think I'm worried? Just look at you, it's not normal, could you explain if I asked you questions about your face?' Ella said, now talking faster, 'Could you tell me why you're so tense? With so much tension around you it's enough to give someone a headache. Chloe, you don't know how much it's upsetting me to see you change into a completely different person, you're not the same person I met,' she said; now it was my turn to say something. I stopped the car and looked at her knowing I would say something rational. I did not want to argue back, I just looked at her.

'Ella I have no answers to give you. I should have told you, I went to see Doctor Harvey as you said I should, he said it could be anxiety so there is nothing to worry about,'

31

she finally cracked out of her moodiness but her face only changed ever so slightly.

As we got to the diner to sit down and order our meals, Ella still looked sad; then I remembered her mum saying about bad news today. 'El please help me out here, if you tell me I may be able to help,' I said trying to be reasonable.

'You won't understand Chloe,' said El, looking serious once again.

'Please. I'm sure it can't be as bad as what I'm going through,' I said trying to convince her it was ok to talk.

The waitress served us our food, I had steak again and of course Ella had salad. 'I had a phone call from college, they dropped me off the course. Oh my, Chloe, your eyes!' at this point I felt that something was happening to me that could change things forever.

She stood up in horror and backed away out towards the door. 'You stay away from me, just leave me alone, and stay away,' Ella shouted in a struggle to speak.

I was stunned for a split second and dashed out of my seat to follow her, 'Ella,' I shouted. 'Ella please wait,' I shouted at the top of my voice. 'Look at me, it is me your friend Chloe,' I said, disappointed.

Ella then turned to face me in the car park, 'Ok, explain this to me, your eyes have turned into something I have never seen before; they are a vibrant green, your pupils look like cats' eyes. It was like, as soon as the food is on the table, it happened,' she said, trembling the words out.

I didn't know what to say, I just looked at her, feeling a strange emotion that took over me, with tears flowing down my pale skin. 'You're not the same person, you have changed. You're a freak to me now, stay away!' she said, now being very serious. I took a deep breath to relax myself, I knew Ella could get very stroppy but I'd never witnessed her have a blow-out like this.

A shocking strong scent I recognised drifted from the other side of the car park, I looked to the direction of the scent and there it was: the truck. I couldn't believe it was him, I could smell the beautiful scent before I could see him. I wanted to go over and confront him to see why I always saw him at the right time and place, whenever I was feeling really stressed he'd appear. He took my breath away. I was drowning in his scent. Ella, at this point, had left me, getting in a taxi and throwing me an evil glare as she left. I quickly got in my car to get home before something else happened. As I was driving home I realised that I could see better in the dark than before. It was incredible. Somehow I wasn't as shocked at these bizarre changes in me anymore. They were beginning to feel natural, like destiny. I was beyond caring. Until I remembered that I had plans to talk to Jane when I got home. I realised I was ready, ready to hear the truth.

I pulled up outside Aunt Jane's house and walked up the steps through the porch into the house, Jane was sitting waiting for me next to a dim lamp with her sketch book on her lap. The lounge was a small cosy room with pictures of Jane's family. I noticed only my uncle and my mum in a photo. My mother was Jane's sister in-law. I sat down in the armchair opposite to Jane. I looked around the cosy room again at the paintings of wild animals, that showed the more sinister side of each creature.

'Aunt Jane, what happened to my mum?' I asked sadly. She smiled and look at me remorsefully.

'I don't know honey, I wish I did, I do think of your beautiful mother; I wish I could tell her what an amazing daughter she has got,' she said peacefully.

'There is one other thing I want to know: what the hell is happening to me? It's crazy I just need to know; I cannot control my emotions. And how come Ben has left?' I said with a raised voice as I could feel my heart pumping faster and faster.

'Chloe, sooner or later it will all become clear, your life is more precious than others, you won't think so now but you soon will,' Jane spoke with a sly grin on her face.

'It doesn't make sense; how do you know this information?' I said, starting to shake, but this time wasn't the same as before, even my head felt like it was going to twist any minute.

'Of course I know, I know everything, but it has to be destiny for you to wait and find the answers for yourself. Only you can pick the path you choose to take, this is your time Chloe, don't fight it, go with it,' she said with excitement.

That was it. With my heart pounding fast, with my hands shaking rapidly, I was getting the answers in a way, but it wasn't good enough and made me feel worse, made me angry, sick, like I was suffocating on the same air she breathed.

I stood up and pushed the sketches off her lap onto the floor and stormed out into the night. I knew that I had to go to my calming place even if I was scared of the forest. I should at least try and run or walk it off on my own.

Before I got in my car, I looked back through the lounge window at Aunt Jane; she was just sat there, calm, with no expression on her face. It got to me even more that she was so laid back. *I have to leave as quickly as possible before I have a break down.* I started driving along with my feet pushing flat on the accelerator, trying to keep an even closer eye on the road. I went to change the track playing, to listen to music to calm me and keep my head clear. Still driving fast, I dropped a disk on the floor; my instant reaction was to pick the disk up. As I leaned over I let go of the wheel. It all happened very suddenly, I felt the car drifting over the road at a high speed. I hit the barrier and smashed into it.

My head hit the window so hard I passed out, after that I had no idea what happened to me. I came round somewhere deep in the forest, I woke up in pain, the shaking was out of control, I couldn't focus on what was going on with my body. I felt my muscles pulsing, getting bigger and stronger. My bones started to click out of my joints, the agonising pain felt like it could kill me, in my mind I wanted to be dead. I no longer had control over my mind; I kept trying to stop the fit. I was still shaking so much that I hit my head extremely hard again.

Black Legend

Within seconds I was filled with the most pain I'd ever experienced in all my life put together. I wasn't myself anymore, it was more than an accident that night; it was nothing I had ever expected to happen.

I finally got up to move, then I realised that my body had changed. My eye sight - I could see in the dark as clear as day. My skin was no longer smooth; I was covered in silky black fur. From that moment, I knew I wasn't human. I was ... well, not human, like some kind of creature. 'Help!' I shouted, but no words escaped my lips. I needed to see what had happened to me, I felt sick and light headed again.

Still sore, I walked down the hill deeper into the forest. It was weird that I was so low to the ground as I pushed myself through the undergrown ferns. My sight had a silver, metallic glow; my sense of smell was unbelievably sensitive, so much so that I could pick up smells from yards away, possibly miles. I didn't feel so stressed and tensed, I felt free, like the way I did when I ran. I began getting deeper into the forest, finding a lake with the moonlight shining down upon it.

The sight was breath taking, *it looks like a picture*. I took a step closer to look at my reflection in the water, I had to prepare myself before I took a look, and it was the most impressive moment I could ever imagine. As I looked down my heart missed a beat. I was incredibly beautiful and magnificent, my ears were small and pointed up, my nose was flat, and I had very long whiskers. My eyes seemed even more vibrant green next to the black fur, teeth pointy and piercing white and sharp. The transformation was a shock. I realised, as purely as I ever thought before, *this is me and I'm not dreaming*. My muscles were so stocky, I felt unbelievably strong. I started to feel strange; that I was far too calm, *how can I possibly go back? What if I don't turn back*? My emotions felt strange again, I got confused with how I felt with this emotion. I couldn't explain how my deep thoughts were telling me, my instincts were saying to me, 'Stay where I am 'til morning.' Aunt Jane must have been worried by now, but I guessed that as she apparently knew everything she would understand. I could see the fish swimming around in the huge lake, I was hungry but I didn't think I could stomach raw fish. I lay down longer, looking at my reflection in fascination 'til I got bored, I started to walk round the mile-long lake; and it was still so peaceful. There were lots of bushes around the lake covering the view into the forest; it was just an empty footpath to go around the lake. I didn't want to go far as it could be risky. I found a resting point to get some rest before dawn.

I fell asleep so quickly, dreaming of that day in the forest when I was running from something that had been watching me. But in this dream it was the mysterious guy that I thought was following me, he was there, as gorgeous as ever. He walked right up towards me and looked into my eyes. I could feel him breathing on my skin, it was so warming. He brushed my hair off my face so gently that I couldn't feel him do so, so passionately. His eyes looked so intensely at mine I felt my heart stop beating for that second, he then grabbed me tightly pulling my waist to his, and then sadly I woke up. I never wanted the dream to end but I was pleased it wasn't a nightmare for a change.

I came round from my deep sleep and I realised I was in my human form, I felt very confused that it didn't hurt as I changed back. It was a beautiful day, the sun beaming down on me, which made me feel even hotter. I climbed to my feet and felt unbalanced as I was walking on four legs the last time I moved; as I gathered my clothes from last night I noticed they were torn, it wouldn't look suspicious as I did have a car crash. I started heading up the hill to where the crash was, it felt a long way compared to last night. I could see my paw prints in the dirt, I covered the prints just in case there were hikers.

I got to my car, it looked awful. I didn't know how I would explain why I was gone all night. *I'm sure I will think of something as I have been telling lies easily the past week, sadly.* I had a really steep hill to climb to get up to the broken barrier, it was difficult. I grabbed hold of the long grass that wasn't tended to, which made it easier. I walked along the side-road to get back home; I knew it was going to be a long trek. I couldn't believe how great I felt. *It's amazing, I feel like a new person, as if I'm on a high.* This was the best I'd felt since my mum died, it was like I'd been living in the dark all this time. A couple drove past, staring at me, I guessed they had reason to, as I had dirty and ripped clothes with a smile on my face, who wouldn't find that something to look at? I had been walking for hours with no one offering a lift, but I wasn't far from Aunt Jane's house. It was the first house you got to once you passed the small bridge over the river just further up.

I took a deep breath as I walked up to the house; I looked up and saw Jane sat on the porch steps outside the front door. 'Morning Jane,' I said trying to go in without questioning from Jane.

'And where do you think you're going?' Jane said, not very pleased.

'Um, I'm just going for a shower,' I said casually,

'Wait, go inside and sit down will you?' she said strictly. So I did exactly as she said. I knew I was in trouble, 'Chloe where we're you last night? And where is your car?' Jane said, stood in front of me with her arms crossed looking straight at me.

'I…um…one, had a car crash and two, passed out and three, woke up in the morning, is that ok? Or don't you believe me like everyone else lately?' I said with a lot of attitude in my voice. Then I smiled at Jane.

Jane looked in shock that I was smiling at her. Even I was shocked that I was smiling. *It feels great smiling* - I'd been doing so since that morning when I woke up. *I think Jane knows exactly what happened last night*, maybe that's why she didn't say anything back to me and dropped the subject.

'Can I make you something to eat Chloe while you're in the shower?' Jane said looking quite pleased with herself for some reason.

'Um, yeah that would be great! Thanks,' I said, extremely jolly. I went upstairs had my shower and was now ready to face the day for a new beginning. I ate my food extremely fast and was out the door in no time. I heard Aunt Jane telling me to be careful on the way out the door. I didn't pay attention to any of this, I was more focused on finding out a bit more about my wild side. I found a close entrance to the forest and started running, *it feels different, I feel stronger and healthy so amazingly not human,* I thought.

The wind was two times faster through my hair than before; my body was strong like steel and felt as fast as a horse. I started to think how everything made sense about the doctors, my scent and how I'd changed so drastically. I just couldn't justify why I was so happy and how I was not so scared. My heart felt in the right place for once. I found the place I was last night, it looked more spectacular than last night. There was far more to look at, I must still have been adjusting to my new eye sight last night, that's why I might not have seen it.

The lake was far more than basic then, now it was spectacular, wild flowers ranged in all different colours and shapes; at the back of the lake was a small but a perfect waterfall that had fairly fast moving water. Massive rocks that were shaped to perfection lay nearby. It was a perfect place to go, where I could escape the modern world, miles away from any neighbourhood so it was perfect not to be seen in.

Wondering, and trying to work out how I would change back into the spectacular monster I became, I knew I wasn't evil enough to be called a monster but I had no other word or meaning to describe it. I wondered why I was so unique, and if anyone knew anything like me existed.

It was a hot day and the sun was shining down on me, I just had to cool off as I could feel my fair skin burning but it wasn't red or sore. I decided to swim in the lake, I stripped down to my underwear and dipped my toe in the water. It was very cold but felt really refreshing. I took a deep breath and dived into the water, as I hit the water, the shock of the cold changed me. It happened within a split second, the pain was over fast, last night was so painful that I could not make sense of how it happened. As I was swimming around, feeling a bit odd doing doggie paddle rather than swimming, I felt young again. It was like I was reborn when I was in my new form.

I got close to the waterfall and jumped onto a rock on the side, it wasn't very easy but I got up in the end. I looked around, with no one in sight it was incredibly blissful, alone. That moment felt so unreal, before I could even think or move I had this strange feeling someone was nearby, I looked around but there wasn't anyone in sight; I even looked up in the tall trees which surrounded the lake. I could smell the scent nearby, it smelled peculiar but innocent.

It was too late to react. I was tied up and knocked unconscious before I got to see who was there. I regained consciousness on a bed and was no longer tied. I had a sheet covering my naked body, with my clothes in a pile at the end of my bed; the door was open so I knew I was not a prisoner.

The room had stone walls and felt slightly damp with oil lamps; the room was very bizarre as there was no electricity that I could see. The room looked like a boy's room. I had a feeling that whoever lived there had been there for a long time, the furniture and fabric looked old and dated. I heard talking and madness going on in a different room, I put my clothes on and walked through a stone corridor. I poked my head round the corner to listen but I soon realised there were more than just one or two people.

'Hi,' I said, being shy but wary at the same time.

'Hey take a seat,' this one guy told me. I was paying attention to how they looked at me, just acting as calm and careful as I could at the same time.

'Chloe it's me,' said the guy sat opposite me. I took a deep and hard look; I couldn't recognise who he was but something seemed familiar.

'Um, I'm sorry but I don't recognise you,' I said trying not to sound rude.

'Chloe it's me Ben, I suppose you wouldn't recognise me. As you know yourself we do change a lot when we hit the right age,' Ben said, laughing at me.

I was shocked and shaking, I did not react straight away. Ben looked completely different, he was a lot taller and had extremely big muscles with a healthy figure, his hair was long and tied back off his face, with green eyes. It was the first time I had seen Ben with long hair.

'Wow, oh my goodness that can't be you! You - um - you look great,' I said, surprised.

'Chloe you must be more careful outside, but you are safe here,' he said with the smile disappearing from his face.

'How do you know it was me Ben? And what happened?' I said, being curious. He just looked at me then smiled.

'Have you ever heard of the "black legends"?' he said with a soft voice.

'The black what?' I said bluntly, I had never heard of them before.

'Chloe listen closely as I'm about to tell you about the black legends,' Ben said.

'Ok go ahead,' I replied and took a seat on the floor. The room had a very different vibe. *I have goose-bumps.*

'The black legends some may call us, or say it's what we are and is in our blood,' Ben stopped for a second and three other men walked into the room and sat on the floor, one I recognised was Tim.

'This is our pack Chloe; you were destined to find us here. We inherited this gene which makes us unique, many generations ago our ancestors were called the "night watchers". They would protect the forest villagers at night with their brilliant eye sight to protect them from the evil that lurks in the night. The pack would pace around the village 'til daylight, the villagers would look up to the legends for their bravery and believe them to be half-human, half-spirit. Only men were night watchers. Some children have phased before men but we don't know why yet, we are still researching. You may not realise yet how powerful and different you are Chloe; you see there were never female black legends, or those known to the human eye as "panthers". Female panthers are so unknown they are more a myth, but still hunted. The female hormones have more emotion than the male and so females are more likely to be more protective. That gives you more strength and incentive to succeed in war,' Ben said, going into more depth.

I was listening very carefully but couldn't get any words out to speak, it was all too much to absorb. 'You must be careful Chloe, there are enemies that come from time to time, and they are not who they seem. Even though you are practically a myth you are very much in danger,' Ben sounded aggressive as he screwed his nose up.

The Pack

This was the most incredible few days I had ever had. I had just found out I was a black panther (a night watcher) I also had been reconnected with my cousin Ben. It also came to my attention that I had been living a long secret that had been kept from me, I wasn't sure how to react now, or it could have been more the fact that I was in a room surrounded by men who were all very attractive, apart from Ben of course.

'Hey Chloe, how are you doing?' Tim said, looking at me with a smile on his face.

'I'm ok thank you, how come you never told me?' I said, frowning at him.

'Chloe I had no choice, it's not a good thing to tell someone if they don't know. You would have not believed me anyway,' said Tim, smiling.

'I would like to introduce every one,' Ben said, and all of a sudden the door to the hidden home flung open. A tall man who was older than the others walked in, he was very largely built, he had bigger muscles than all of us put together; his hair was jet black with a few white hairs and was styled very short. 'Ah just in time,' said Ben, the tallest guy then came and sat down on a chair in the corner by the oil lamp. 'I'd like to introduce your new family, friends and pack. You know Tim already, he's our provider. Then you've got Brad, he's the eyes and ears of this pack, he likes to watch the lake,' Ben said pointing over to Brad. Brad was short and stocky with dark hair and green eyes with pale skin. I was starting to see a connection between us all. 'And I'd like to introduce Rob who is our messenger.' Once again dark hair, but blue eyes with slightly less paleness.

'He passes on when danger is on the way,' Ben now looked towards the big chap sitting in the arm chair.

'Now this is Adam, he is our leader, what he says goes now Chloe. And it's the same for every other watcher,' Ben smiled.

'Hey I'm not that bossy Ben. Sorry Chloe, they may call me the leader but I am more of a guardian. I will keep you safe, as long as you listen to me you won't get hurt,' Adam said seriously. All the others had a grin on their faces. I couldn't tell whether they were happy just to have new company, or if it was the fact that I was female.

'Ben let's get her trained into shape, you must teach Chloe everything she needs to know to survive,' said Adam, now giving orders. I'm thinking to myself, *what is Ben, what is his position?*

'Just one question I have to ask, what does Ben do exactly?' I said genially, wondering.

'Ha ha,' the others laughed out loud.

'Hey guys you know I'm in the best position of the pack. Chloe, I do the training around here making sure these idiots keep in shape,' said Ben, admonishing the others for laughing at him.

'Well I guess that is important, there isn't much to do in the middle of the forest,' I started to think there was a catch to this.

'Ben doesn't just do training, oh no he is the tracker, no one has a nose like him, and Ben has the sense that can pick up anything. It's very uncommon,' said Adam. *I thought panthers all together were uncommon*, I joked to myself.

'So what would I do then if I come and visit?' I said, just out of interest.

'Visit?' Adam and Tim shouted.

'Sorry Chloe you are part of our pack now you have to stay with us,' Ben said, as if it would be a crime not to.

'Well what about Aunt Jane? I can't just leave her it's not fair,' I said sadly.

'And you think it was easy for me? Well think again Chloe, leaving mum is the hardest thing I had to do. I didn't want her to get hurt, mum not knowing my whereabouts is for the best,' Ben said.

Now this just confused me even more, my head just could not handle and take it all in and I decided it was just better to co-operate with them.

'Ok I will stay but just for now and then, to start with,' I said, compromising. I could not help but think I was doing a bad thing at that moment not being with Jane.

'Ready Chloe?' Ben said in excitement.

'Ready for, what exactly?' I said in confusion, with a grin on my face.

'Ready to see what we have got? They don't call us legends for no reason,' Ben said, with the others in the background play fighting, while Adam just sat in his chair looking embarrassed at Brad and Tim fighting.

'Bring it on; apart from the fact that I have no clue what I'm doing,' I said, with a smile on my face that was starting to hurt my face, as I was still not used to smiling.

'Ha ha course you don't know what you're doing, that's why I'm teaching you silly,' Ben said, laughing.

We both walked over to the front door, I looked back at the others to say bye but no one was paying attention. 'Chloe this maybe a bit difficult for you as the water comes down hard,' Ben said seriously. I didn't understand a thing he said until he opened the door, the loud noise of the back of the waterfall was behind the stone wall. I had no idea that this was where they made their hide out, I thought that I was in a stone cabin hidden deep into the forest, little did I know.

'You need to hold your breath as you dive down, next you need to gradually breath out when out go under the water fall, once the water looks clear and stiller then we can make our way up, you got that?' Ben instructed me.

'Yea think so...' I was about to say, until Ben went ahead and dived in. I waited a couple of seconds so I could recap Ben's instructions. I jumped high in the air and dived in; the water was very cold and dark where the waterfall forcefully joined the lake. It took a lot of my strength to swim through the force of the 'fall. I slowly let air out of my nose to keep me under water deeper. It worked well. The fish made me jump as I got closer to clear water, and the lake was pure and clean water. The lake almost looked like a bath with fish in.

I got to the bay at the other end of the lake and climbed out, it was horrible being in wet clothes. Ben gave me a wave to get a move on; he seemed worried for some reason.

I walked over to him, 'You ok? You look a bit tense,' I said to my cousin.

'Yes all good, we need to get a move on before dark,' Ben said seriously. *But I've been here at dark and I've never sensed trouble,* I thought.

'How come?' I wondered.

'People think we come out at night, the myth says we can only see in dark,' Ben explained.

'But we *can* see in dark; do people know about the black legend,' I asked in horror. He just stopped and looked at me.

'There is nothing to worry about, like you said, it's a myth, and we like to keep our pack that way.' Ben was now getting agitated as we carried on conversing. 'Here,' Ben shouted.

'Wow this is some place,' I said in shock.

I looked around at this massive ring of space surrounded by big boulders and trees around the edges, the ground was dusty and soft. I could see massive paw prints in the dusty dirt. 'Hey,' I shouted to Ben. 'Whose are these paw prints? They are huge, bigger than mine,' I said, worrying. I wasn't sure if I wanted the answer, it could have been a big, dangerous animal to be afraid of.

'They're mine Chloe, I spend a lot of time here training myself,' Ben said with a sly grin. 'Let's get started, I hope you can keep up,' Ben shouted.

'I will try, but I'm not fast on my feet,' I said.

'Who says you'll be on your feet,' then Ben laughed.

'But how can I change, I don't know how to?' I was confused.

'Ok it's easy once you have found your trigger, could be anger, sadness or a strange emotion. It is what you get before you change, you need to use it,' Ben said as if it was easy.

I began thinking back to when the phase first happened, the pain and anger I felt. But my strange emotion only happened when there was a change in my life, like the car accident, maybe that change triggered the other change. I took a deep, hard look into my past back to when I was in England.

There was a memory that popped into my head; *I was at the park on a swing, my mum was pushing me. My mum looked similar to myself but older, she was happy and smiling with a perfect set of teeth and plump lips. Me and mum were laughing while dad watched, sat on a bench, he had a smile ear to ear. All of a sudden dad's face dropped, he noticed the tall man behind us dressed in black, and mum noticed and grabbed me and covered my eyes. I could just about remember the noise I could hear, 'We can do this the easy way or the hard way,' the stranger said to dad.*

'Take Chloe some place safe now,' dad said to my mum, he sounded so worried. I didn't know what happened after that, it was such a long time ago. I did know that dad came home that night in a wreck, he looked

like he was attacked. Mum went straight over to him to hold him, the door closed and I could hear them talking about the stranger in the park. I was too young to realise my family was in danger.

'Hey Chloe, you ok?' Ben said as I came round from day dreaming.

'Sorry Ben, I think I know my trigger, what happens after?' I said, worrying.

'I want you to copy my every move, you will communicate through my body expressions,' Ben wasn't very good at taking time to explain things in more detail.

'Ok I will try,' I said. Ben climbed up a huge rock, he stopped and stood tall, then he leapt into the air towards the other rock. As he was leaping he changed into the most beautiful creature I'd ever seen, the transition was quick, in a blink of an eye he wasn't the Ben I knew. His muscles around his shoulder bulked out, he looked extremely strong, his coat was a shiny jet black that in some lights had a blue tone. Ben was no longer Ben, he looked dangerous. His eyes were metallic green like mine. Ben also had claws that looked and sounded as sharp as kitchen knives.

All of a sudden he looked at me and roared, I realised he was saying it was my turn to change. I would be in trouble if I didn't try to phase, just looking at him scared me. I had never seen a panther, only my reflection of course. He moved with ease and looked light on the ground, tail rocking either side with simple strides.

I climbed up the rock; it looked bigger as I was climbing. As I got to the top I started to think of things to get that emotion back: I had flashbacks of falling out with

Ella, Aunt Jane's grin, and the doctor forcing me to leave. I could feel it now, my body hurt so badly. The muscles tearing with a burning sensation like it was tearing under my flesh, my gums stretching as I felt my teeth move and grow. I fell from the rock by accident, I felt my body shrink and for a second I blacked out while I was falling, then I landed on all four legs.

I felt so amazing, so dangerous, that the power was getting to me. The change was getting less painful and quicker. Ben stopped, as I caught up with him, he started running pretty fast.

I was struggling to keep up with him but I had to keep going; he was getting faster and faster. All of a sudden he jumped on and off the tree trunks as if he was bouncing off them one by one, he was so quick that I could just make out where he had gone. It looked like a black cloud moving fast in the air; it was my turn to try. I kept my speed up and leapt up at a tree trunk with force. To my disappointment, I fell back to the ground again, it was not so easy; so I tried again. Every tree trunk I got to I failed to jump from, Ben looked back at me, I sensed disappointment. My speed was fine; it was my strength that made me weaker than the others. I could understand why I was not in fit condition, but by the look of Ben he couldn't.

He suddenly stopped sharp, I stuck my paws down hard into the ground so I didn't go into him. The force from my speed made me skid through the dirt, leaving marks in the ground. Ben turned around and headed back towards the training ground. I ran back to follow him, but he was gone, too quick to catch up to this time. I got to the training ground where I saw Ben back in his human form;

he was zipping his jacket up. Ben looked and pointed to behind the rock,

'Think of happy thoughts,' Ben said. As I got behind the rock I saw my clothes in a neat pile, *ok I must think happy*. I thought hard to see when I last felt happiness. I closed my eyes and tilted my head down towards the ground. *Ah that's it, it's him that made me feel warm inside.* His face looking at me, his scent that sent me wild wanting more. His presence was enough to get me shy and nervous, but at the same time it was a good feeling. I blacked out for a few seconds and came round as a human; I wondered to myself if the others blacked out. I got dressed and went back round to see Ben.

'Chloe, up here!' Ben shouted. He was sat on the huge rock.

I climbed up to meet him, he didn't look very pleased. 'What's wrong? Is it me or...' I said, confused.

'Please listen to me, what I have to tell you, for your own good,' Ben said with emotion in his big eyes.

'Ok, of course I will listen,' I said, feeling worried.

'Look I didn't want you to get involved with this, I said to Adam, its strength of the pack not numbers,' Ben was now looking around checking we were alone. 'But you see he thinks that a female is just what we need, I don't want to lose faith in you. But it's not safe for you here, there are others on the way,' Ben looked at me, straight in the eyes.

'Hang on you said others? Like pack members, right?' I felt a slight sting listening to this.

'Others that are different, unique; we try to research them but there is nothing to trace, we don't know anything about them, only that they are new breed and could be superior to us. Parts from stories about the black legends say females are supposed to be wise and quick learners,' Ben was now starting to scare me. 'Chloe, Adam thinks you're the one to save us from extinction, but from what I see today, we might as well just be extinct right now.' Ben really hurt me, but he sounded stupid.

'Hang on a second, I found out a day ago I am this creature, and now you expect me to know everything. I can just about get used to walking, not fighting or jumping trees and things,' I said aggressively. I was getting angry again and my heart was racing.

'You're right, I'm sorry, it is very difficult; we don't know how long we've got left for training. I don't want you to get hurt,' Ben looked away again.

'I won't, I have the right trainer for the job,' I said, smiling at him to cheer him up.

He jumped down from the rock and I followed, he and I both knew there was no way out of this. I couldn't help but think on the way back, *is this destiny and my responsibility to defend a part of me I know nothing about?* I felt dark inside as my thoughts were now troubling. I had no idea what we were up against or if I had it in me to keep up with the others, *is Adam going to let me back out if I want?* I thought to myself.

Once again I felt there was something kept from me, like more secrets building up to uncover. We got to the lake, the walk back was really quiet as Ben didn't say a word. I stopped as he was heading to the edge of the lake, when: 'Come on, time to eat,' Ben said.

'I better get back to Jane as she is going to be worrying,' I said, looking to the ground knowing that he would be disappointed.

'Why, it's not like she will be worried about you right?' he said with rage. I couldn't work out why he and Jane didn't like to talk, or even the fact that he left.

'At least I'm there for your mum, I know she misses you,' I said to stand up for her.

'Stay out of this Chloe before it's too late for you, you know Adam won't be happy about you not staying,' he said as he walked away from me. I couldn't leave on bad terms.

'I will see you tomorrow,' I said to keep him sweet.

I could feel in my heart walking away was a bad choice, knowing that we had enemies after us. Too much had happened in one day that my little brain couldn't handle. I decided to run back home before it got dark, *it may do me good to run off the tension*. I began feeling good being in the forest on my own. I felt my heart pounding faster and faster, I was running the same speed a horse would do when cantering. My speed kept getting better and better, to a point where I wondered how I would stop running.

As I got to the quiet road I started to walk back home, I felt extremely odd, as in one day: I'd found my cousin Ben, I'd learned about the black legends and I'd learned that they had some kind of fight for existence, and if that wasn't enough to overwhelm me then I definitely was not human. I wanted to find out more about the female black legends and how I could prove to Adam that I was willing to be part of the pack without living with them. I couldn't even imagine what it would be like living with six men, would I have to do chores and cook for them as well as train?

I was back at Jane's, as I walked up the front garden path I could see Jane looking out of the kitchen window. She looked surprised to see me, like I was a ghost from the past. I walked through the front door and looked around. Something looked different from when I left earlier. I took a good look around, Aunt Jane walked through the door into the main room.

'Hello Chloe how was your day?' she said very strangely. I couldn't suss her out, why she was being odd with me, I could sense danger here, it was a really unpleasant feeling. Jane had been acting oddly with me since the changes, I realised, and I started to wonder if Ben was warning me away from Aunt Jane.

'Yes I've been running all day thank you,' I said hoping she would believe me. She looked at me again and sat down in her arm chair. She then got her sketchbook and started drawing.

I went upstairs to my room, my room, since this morning, looked odd, different - things had been moved. I couldn't see what had gone as I had a lot of clutter in boxes under my bed and on the desk.

I began to rush around like a headless chicken, I had to act fast before Jane caught me tearing my room apart. But I had so much stuff I couldn't know what had changed. Instinctively, I looked in my personal box under my bed. The box was completely empty, only a photo of me and my mum and dad was left, my birth certificate, my school reports, my baby photos, passport and my driving license were all missing. I could feel my head nearly exploding and panic building up in my chest.

My strange emotion was nearly taking control of me. I had to stop myself from changing I had no idea what to do; I guessed I had to reverse the emotion before it was too late. I restrained myself on my bed; I would lose, and my body would be in total control if I didn't contain my feelings in a second. I took a deep breath and thought of all my happy places in my mind, like when I was in England with my mum, she was pushing me on the swing, I couldn't stop giggling because I found it so fun, and the strange man wasn't there. I could feel my body gradually calm down, my body staying still. That was rather hard to stop but I knew one day I wouldn't be able to control it and it scared me a lot.

It was very difficult to know what to do with my life now, I couldn't stay here, I could be in danger. Aunt Jane could be dangerous to me. The confusion made me so emotional, knowing that someone could be stalking me and that my existence was in danger. I now didn't feel safe, I felt on edge all the time. I was beginning to think that Adam was right, I should be there. I would have to see how I felt in the next two days, as the choice could risk my life and also risk others. This decision could be something that my life depended on.

I will find the person who has stolen all the proof of identity and that I exist and they will pay for what they have done. I packed my stuff and took what I had left that was important, I felt extremely unsafe at Jane's house. Something was different; I sensed that I was near evil. It felt odd not knowing why I felt like this, I looked outside and Jane was talking to a stranger out the back, with a black hooded jacket on, he had his hood up and was standing at such an angle that the hood hid his face. I opened the window lightly without making a sound, to see if I could smell his scent.

I recognised the scent; it didn't have the same effect on me as the scent of the man I had seen outside the doctor's practice had. It gave me the effect of anger, but a passionate anger; I dropped my bags. I decided that I should stay and learn more about Aunt Jane. I was frightened but even worse, confused.

The One

Two months later, things were different. Winter was on its way, Aunt Jane was still being different towards me and the stranger was around often. I was at the campsite most days and training with Ben before nightfall. Adam was still trying to convince me that it was not safe to be apart from the pack. Little did he know that I knew I wasn't safe to be away from the pack after nightfall.

I had no sightings of the man in the black truck, apart from in my dreams. I woke up smiling to the sweet dream of him most mornings, the smile soon faded as reality hit me like morning breath.

'Chloe,' shouted Aunt Jane.

'Coming,' I replied with a fake sweet voice for my estranged aunt. As I got myself together and went downstairs, Aunt Jane was in the kitchen looking into the refrigerator. I found it hard to look at her ever since I had seen through her kind facade.

'We need more food, you have eaten us dry, are you some kind of eating machine?' she said, staring at me without a blink. I was lost for words; I had been since the day she got sneaky.

'Run down the supermarket and refill what you have eaten,' she said.

Once again words struggled to fall out my mouth, 'Ok,' was the only amount of conversation I could say these days. I managed to get myself a new car second hand, it was not as smart as my other one but it was all I could afford. The pack needed me and Tim to help with food and equipment as the others broke a lot of things after over-excitement. I left the house without a word, I could sense Jane was up to something.

The joy of leaving the house was like being out of hell. It had been two months, and still I was no closer to any discovery. It was a half hour journey to the nearest supermarket. I didn't have much money on me but just enough to keep Jane happy. My mobile phone was ringing as I was driving, I answered with my hands-free, more cautious after my accident.

'Chloe, it's Ben,' Ben sounded upset.

'What's going on?' I said, surprised he called.

'Don't go home, please don't go back there just promise me you won't,' Ben was shouting hysterically.

'Calm down, you know I can't,' I said, feeling bad that I couldn't tell him what was going on at home.

'My mum. I've just seen her with some guy; he's one of them,' he said, confusing me.

'Look I don't know what you're going on about, one of whom exactly?' I said.

'Just meet me back at the caves,' he replied.

'I'm on my way to get food for Jane, I'll call you back,' then I hung up.

I didn't want to know what dangers were about when I was driving away, out of reach. I was having to control my strange emotion as I trembled while driving. I could tell by Ben's voice it was serious. I got to the supermarket, luckily it was hardly busy; as I got myself a big trolley and walked through the doors everyone was looking and I felt nervous. I thought to myself that I should get the shopping done as fast as I could. The shop was very cold, the air conditioning was amazing, leaving me feeling refreshed. I was trying to remember what I had eaten; *I don't think that I have been eating like a machine.* Someone had, but I ate mostly at the waterfall cave. But, not to be suspicious, I had to do the shopping. I carried on down each aisle picking up the essentials, I felt more embarrassed and awkward with myself as I got to the meat counter. The smell made my mouth water, I couldn't focus myself to think about what I needed. Something else smelt delicious, the scent was getting stronger and stronger and my quick reflexes made me turn round.

'Huh,' I gasped with shock, was it him or was I dreaming? Nope, definitely not dreaming. He looked so amazing close up. I could not speak and didn't know what to say, my bright green eyes were just glaring at him. I could have fainted from the strong heat of the moment.

'Hello, I'm sorry, I didn't mean to spook you like that,' he said to me. His voice was so gentle and his words felt powerful, he smiled like butter wouldn't melt. I had to speak but I was worried I would say something silly.

'Hi,' I did it. I couldn't even say more.

'What is your name?' he asked, I was getting the shakes and butterflies. *Uh oh, no not now*, I thought.

'Chloe,' I said, really quiet and shy.

'My name is Charlie,' he said. My head went funny; I was getting a sharp pain in my head. And just like that, when I thought the worst was over, the room went dark and I collapsed to the floor, I must have fainted.

I woke up in his truck, I came round with my head against the passenger's window; I felt really awkward. I looked in the back and saw my shopping in bags, 'Thank you,' I managed to slip out from between my lips. The sweet scent could have knocked me off my feet all over again. *Charlie looks so serious when he is driving*, I noticed, his body posture looked uneasy, as if he was not sure what he was doing. I could not help but look at his perfect muscly arms, how his face was so perfectly shaped. He didn't say a word for a while, I could tell that he was thinking of words to say to not make me feel spooked.

'I will help you with your shopping, and then when you're feeling... less faint we will get your car,' Charlie said in his husky voice. He was like my knight in shining armour coming to save the day. I must have been still dreaming, if I wasn't then my first impression was awful. That would be one to remember, passing out on the poor guy.

'That would be great,' I said lightly, trying to make up for a bad first appearance. The truck had so much tension you could cut it with a knife. It was so nice just to be in the company of someone who didn't expect anything from me. The pack and Jane were the only people I saw; Ella still wouldn't talk to me.

It'd been very different in the past month, so different that I hadn't thought about Ella before this moment. *I do miss her dizziness, and the bombshell blonde locks.* I should have made more of an effort not to fall out with her and told the truth. "Lies will always bite back at you," my mum used to say. We got to Jane's driveway, she wasn't home which was odd. Charlie never asked for directions, I knew he wouldn't as he had been watching me for some time now.

I looked at him while I thought about my next move. 'Let me give you a hand,' Charlie said. I nodded, knowing that if I said no, he wouldn't take that as an answer. As I opened the door I looked around to check Ben wasn't still on the lookout, luckily, men were not allowed to when training, as it complicated things.

'That would be great if you could,' I said with a wide smile, gazing into his eyes. I started to feel more relaxed around him, but he was still a mystery to me. I got my keys out of my pocket and opened the door ready for Charlie to bring in the shopping. 'Kitchen is on the right,' I said out loud to direct him.

'Where would you like me to put your shopping?' he asked.

'Just on the table thanks,' I replied.

I was starting to feel a natural confidence growing. Following his scent was even more breath-taking. I felt more feelings the longer I was near him.

I started to unpack the shopping; he stood leaning on the wall looking at me. With every movement and smile, his eyes were there watching. 'We finally meet I guess,' I said in a bubbly manner. I looked at him as he stood there with a huge cheeky grin on his face.

'I guess we did,' Charlie said still grinning, his words made goose-bumps appear on my skin.

I was rushing to put the shopping away before Jane got back and caught me with a stranger in the house. As I picked up a bottle to put in the fridge it slipped out of my hands, before I could even realise what had happened, Charlie caught the bottle. I was shocked by his quick reflexes and how he got there so quickly. I didn't say a word as I would only have asked him how he did that. Thoughts started to run through my mind, how quick he was; that one minute he was lent against the wall and then he was over the other side of the kitchen.

The goose-bumps came back, but this time I sensed something else. 'We need to leave,' I said.

It was Jane; I could sense she was near and that things could go from bad to worse for me. 'Ok then, I take it you're ok now,' Charlie said, like he was wondering what I was up to and why suddenly we had to leave.

'Lots better, I will meet you outside,' I quickly replied. I could feel her gaining, closer and closer, step by step. I quickly locked the door and ran to his truck looking around as I did. I could not see anyone but I knew that she wasn't far.

'You ok? You're acting a little bit strange,' he said, looking into my eyes, and my problems just felt like they were melting away.

'I told my aunt I will be out most of the day, we are not getting on so well,' I said as if it was not that interesting me falling out with Jane. He started the engine and reversed out of the drive. As he turned the wheel and left, I could see Jane hiding in the trees in the corner of my sight. I had no idea that she was this close to the house.

I gasped out loud in shock, I could not believe how things had changed so much with Jane. It was impossible to believe that my own aunt could be like this, that this was who my uncle married years ago. *I'm just grateful I don't have the same blood running through my veins*, I thought.

'I knew she was watching us,' he said frowning as he was driving. 'I thought she might be your mum not your aunt,' Charlie said, looking like he was working it all out.

'It's complicated, I live with her now as mum died and dad left me,' I struggled to say without getting agitated.

'Where did you live before?' he asked me.

'In England. I was there up until nearly ten years ago, not long after my uncle passed away.'

I started to feel emotional talking about the past to someone I did not know. The feeling was growing more intense and I felt less in control as the days since I had discovered my power went by.

'Can we change the subject, it brings back bad memories that I wish not to speak of,' I asked, being clear that I would not continue on with the conversation. There was more awkward silence. I could hear him breathing. I felt safe near Charlie, more so than at home. When I was near him things seemed more clear, there was time to think positively.

He turned on his music, he surprised me with the same taste of genre. 'When will I next see you?' Charlie asked desperately, wanting to see me again. I didn't know when was the right time to meet him or to ever see him again. It seemed like destiny was on my side to meet him. But I was not ready to be mixed up with another adventure as a deadly one had already just begun, *but I guess it doesn't hurt to get to know someone I can go to when things get tough. Charlie is addictive, his looks, smile, scent, his voice is all a dream but so real.*

The thought of not seeing his beautiful face was a disappointment. I felt so driven to desire when I looked into his blue eyes, he was so breath-taking.

'Um, I guess I can see you tomorrow when night falls,' I replied, shaking with nerves that made me feel warm inside. I was hoping he would let me down tomorrow, not that I didn't want to see him again but I just got too shy and nervous near him, it was painful to act calm around Charlie.

'Tomorrow late evening is great,' Charlie said, with a smile that could brighten any day, any weather.

I already felt nervous for tomorrow, I'd never been on a date or thought about dating. Dating seemed so official and stereotypical. This was why I never was interested as there were so many reasons not to participate in dates back at school.

Ok, this is really going to happen, I thought to myself. How come I was being so idiotic about this? I was at the age when dates should be easy, still I had no idea where we were going to go and what we would be doing. I turned my face to face Charlie, I had not noticed that his face was looking in my direction, and realised that he was trying to figure out what I was thinking by my facial expressions.

'Well this is my stop,' I said, trying to break the ice, embarrassed.

'I guess I will see you tomorrow,' Charlie said with a grin. He must be thinking I'm shy.

'Ok,' I answered, so quickly that my ok only sounded like 'Kay. 'Thanks, see you,' I said as I jumped out of the truck and closed the door behind me.

As soon as I got into my car I sighed with relief that I was no longer on constant egg shells trying not to fall and make a fool of myself.

Then it hit me so hard that I gasped for breath, *Ben, oh no! He's been waiting for me*. I'd be in so much trouble if I didn't get there fast enough. Without another thought on how it would be when I saw Ben, I quickly turned the ignition on and put my car in drive, I was driving as fast as I could but more carefully than before my accident.

I had no idea why I was so eager to see the pack knowing full well a warm greeting would not be coming my way. I knew that I could not leave my car at Jane's house and leave by foot, it would give away my sneakiness and suspicions, it was a risk I was not willing to make. I drove to the nearest layby, where I went running, it was a lot longer than I was used to to the secret cave but I was fast enough to only be five minutes.

Running was a huge risk in daylight now, but I'd always been careful. My senses were great to detect people nearby or pick up unusual scents, which were normally just hikers. I ran so fast now that the speed made me feel like the ghost of the forest, like a flash of light to the human eye. I wanted to slow down, take a few more moments to think about today. Little did I see that Brad was out on watching duty, and was heading towards my direction. I froze, stood still.

'Chloe, darling, how many times? You don't have to stop and wait, I can recognise your scent from anywhere,' Brad said with a huge grin on his face, trying not to laugh.

'Do I take the scent thing as a compliment or complaint?' I replied seriously, to see if I could wipe that grin off his face. I'd learnt so much about Brad in the past few weeks, I knew that he had the sense of humour of a ten-year-old. He liked to make jokes and make the most of life, he did not see the black legend as a burden. This was why Brad and I had grown to be good friends.

'Take it as a compliment.' Brad then turned his smile upside down.

'What's wrong is everything ok?' Things started to feel tense, if I had had hair on the back of my neck it would have been up on ends at that moment.

'Ben will tell you, it's better we talk as a family on this one Chloe,' he said and turned to walk beside me.

Brad preferred to say family than pack, he said pack sounded like something we had to be in and it didn't describe what we all meant together. Brad never had a family he was always in and out of care, until he realised what he was. It scared him so much that he ran away into the forest, he was there for months until he came across Adam. He must have been as scared as I knew I was. Adam took Brad under his wing and told him everything he needed to know about the black legends. It was understandable why Brad and Adam were close, Brad looked up to Adam. We were still walking not running for some unknown reason, judging by the look on Brad's face he was not in a hurry to see Ben, as much as I was.

'Brad I'm worried,' I said in a low, soft voice, I could even hear my own emotion in my voice.

'What is there to worry about Chloe? You have me and the others,' he sounded convincing but I knew so much more was happening around us.

'You don't understand Brad it's–' I quickly cut off my sentence when I saw Ben running towards us. *We are just a couple of miles away from the cave, what is he doing coming to us?* I thought.

'Chloe where were you? I've been looking everywhere for you, is it all a joke to you?' Ben was shouting at me.

I was shocked, I thought it must have been about me going off with Charlie. Did he see me with him and was that why he was shouting at me?

'Calm down, Ben,' Brad shouted back, looking like he was about to bite Ben's head off. I could feel my adrenaline kicking in, knowing any minute now I was going to go as well. Brad was up in Ben's face when I realised I had to step in quick before a fight broke out.

'Brad step down, out of my face before I–' I cut Ben off as I jumped so quickly between them and pushed them both apart, it was so quick that I didn't even notice I pushed them so hard that they went twenty yards away from me. I looked to Brad in shock; he was sat on the floor laughing in hysterics. I turned to look at Ben, petrified at what his expression would be. But I had no idea that Ben was right behind me. I could feel his breathing go through my hair onto my neck; I didn't want to face him.

'Um, I, um, had no idea that was going to happen, sorry,' I tried to sound like I was not frightened of Ben's reaction.

'Forget about that; we need to talk, alone,' Ben looked straight over to Brad's direction sternly.

'Ok, ok I'm going,' Brad got up, smiled at me, and ran onwards until he was a blur in the distance. Ben walked over to a broken tree trunk and sat on top of it, I followed over to where he was, looking at his dark eyes. I felt his pain in his eyes; he looked like something was eating away at him.

'Um, you know those moments that change your life and you wish you'd never seen or heard?' Ben said, looking to the floor once again, finding it hard to look at me.

'Yeah I think I've had a lot to those moments recently,' I said looking at Ben who was still looking at the floor.

He looked at me, for a minute it was all silent around me, he turned and said, 'Well this is one of those moments.'

A Beautiful Enemy

I gasped and swallowed at the thought of more life changing moments, I wanted to block my ears and pretend I hadn't heard everything Ben said. The forest started to look darker and deeper as night was drawing in.

'First things out the way, what I'm about to tell you is because I have to, I don't want to hurt you or scare you in any way, but we are family.' He looked back to the floor again and I could see water in the corners of his eyes. 'I'm about to be the only family you'll have left in this world, I guess you know already there's something odd with my mum.' He looked back at me, his eyes were dark and watery.

'Yes I know she–' Ben interrupted me.

'Ok so you know some strange people have visited previously.' He was looking around over his shoulder as if he was checking we was alone.

'Yes,' I kept it short so I wouldn't get interrupted again.

'There are people who don't like our existence, they go way back to the time where black legends formed a

71

pack to protect the village from enemies. Very clever people, Chloe, very clever, the enemies were known as "hunters". They frowned upon our ancestors as monsters of the forest, believing that we were dragged out of hell to destroy men and feed from mankind. They had no idea that we were protecting the village people and our ancestors.

'The hunters came across the black legends on a hunting trip into the mountains for their people. When snow fell on the mountains the people struggled to find food to feed their families and decided to travel to dry land in the forest where the deer and wildlife thrived. They set up a group of men to leave for hunting, they were unique and strong men that could run fast and had good eyes, also quick legs that were great for hunting. Hunters are our natural enemy and would do anything they could to put us down, even when they discovered we weren't hurting our own people. Through time we have studied and worked out a pattern, they are very much like humans but are very enduring,' Ben explained.

'The hunters' knowledge has adapted through the years and their running has become fast like ours, so fast that some can out-run us in our other form.' I thought to myself, *why did he not tell me this before? And how do these hunters relate to Aunt Jane?* 'Chloe please listen carefully,' Ben was really finding it hard to tell me this story and I started to understand why. 'They look like normal people with eyes that were in no doubt god's creation; some females are hunters by name but not hunters in life. They also are tall and slim and you don't even need to be close to them to smell the strong scent of these hunters,' I gasped again in horror.

'Tell me more please,' I said to Ben.

'I'm not finished yet, it's only at the beginning,' I took a deep breath before he started again, blocking out the obvious thoughts. 'Myths and stories tell us some male hunters are naturally attractive to female legends; also the same for female hunter's, they are attractive to male legends, they say the feeling is like magnetism the feeling of a positive and negative connecting but if you put a negative and negative near each other they repel, i.e. male hunters and male legends, they automatically feel the need to fight, and find each other repulsive. But they say once connected you can't break off unless they are strong enough to break the connection. I've never been in love nor fallen in love but I reckon if it's wrong to be together you'd use all you had to stop those feelings and turn it into a greater good, you're thinking why did I tell you that love muck for?' Ben looked at me with a frown.

I blushed, I understood more than he knew on the love muck he spoke of. Taking that as a no, he continued. 'You see my dad was one of us. In fact he was a pack leader, an alpha, he stayed youthful, the leader always does until his first child is born, so my mum was in fact that other magnet, which should have repelled but didn't. She was not a hunter by name or by life, but she was from a generation of hunters. She did not have any contact or loyalty with her family for years until my father died on his last change, which broke the connection. I ran away as soon as I could and met Adam. He explained everything to me.

'My mum contacted her family just before he died. I don't know why she did but they found my dad that day, after his many years of peace. And that's what I think is happening to you,' he said, looking out to the dark forest that we could still see. I took a deep breath, hoping this story had a happy ending.

73

'I went to check on you at Jane's house but all I could see was mum talking to one of them in the back yard, she handed the tall person in a black hooded jacket some sort of document,' Ben's face was not looking so sad anymore, he was serious.

I thought to myself, *document?* and realised exactly what it was: 'My passport,' I gasped.

'You know something, don't you?' One of Ben's eyebrows raised.

'Not as much as you do, why the hell would they want my identification?' I raised my voice, this time I wasn't going to calm down it would take all my energy to stop me. Ben looked like he was going to talk, but he seemed to be speechless. 'What's wrong? I need to know Ben,' I carried on, raising my voice and repeated louder.

'They know we are near,' I could just about lip read Ben's lips he was that quiet.

'Who knows? Ben.'

'Hunters, it's bad enough that we've got the new breed after us. But this,' Ben was now putting this in perspective.

This was a day I would never forget, but he was right that it would be one of those moments that would change my life. 'Chloe,' Ben raised his voice trying to pull me out of my thoughts. I didn't want to listen anymore, 'Chloe,' he then tugged my arm, trying harder.

'This is it, isn't it?' I said feeling my emotion starting to overpower my body.

'What do you mean?' he said, trying to work out what my thoughts were leading to.

'We are all doomed,' my leg was starting to twitch and the other leg wouldn't stop moving.

'Control it Chloe, please. Look let's go back to the pack and talk this through together, ok?'

My mind was now bubbling at his idiotic reaction telling me to control it. I didn't want to control this anymore; I was irritated every day having to control this monster within me. This was my time to go off on a rampage, I never got to grips with who I was on my own.

'No,' I turned and looked at Ben.

'Chloe it's not safe to be out here not now and probably not ever,' his voice was even more irritating when he spoke seriously. As I stood up to look at Ben, moving to leave this dreaded conversation, Ben got up to follow. I let out my loudest growl; Ben looked really shocked at my reaction. He almost looked scared. 'If it's like that then go,' Ben shouted.

I turned my back and started to run, within a quick flash of pain and agony I changed into the beautiful monster that dwelt inside of me. This was the world that should not have existed, I never wanted this. To have such a beautiful enemy was not what I wanted; *if I could just go back to when Aunt Jane and I were a team and Ella was still my best friend, then I might fall in love with someone that was not a demon with angel eyes.* I was still running and leaping into a part of the forest I didn't know so well.

The dark night with the owls making music under the star lit sky was beautiful, *I'm nothing but a dark myth lurking around for danger.* Ben's perception of danger was not as close as mine; he was not in as deep as me. Charlie was my magnet that connected with me, and I felt hooked and longed to see him again. I felt drawn with affliction; there were no rights but all wrongs. I wanted this not to be me so badly that I could feel a stabbing pain in my heart. I couldn't stop my thoughts, nor could I stop my four legs from running into the long distance.

Something caught me by surprise and offhand, it was a white mist that shot across the ground; I walked into the bushes to see what this white mist could be. I tried to be really quiet; I couldn't even hear the owls hooting happily in the tall trees. The atmosphere around where I stood was chilling, this time the hair I did have on my back was standing on end. A strange scent shot up my nose, it was very discomforting. The scent was sour and gross like acid burning in my nose. I'd never come across something so foul in the forest before; neither had my weak sense of tracking. This scent would have been easily remembered if I had picked it up before.

My first initiative was to follow this disgusting white mist scent, but the hair on my back told me it was dangerous. It might be worth going to the pack to tell them of my strange experience tonight. I waited for a little while until the scent had faded away, and the tension had disappeared. I followed my own tracks back; it took me longer to find my way there as it was difficult to pick my tracks up from running so fast.

I started to pick up speed with the training and practice I was getting. I got back to where I left; I picked up my clothes with my teeth and put them in a nice pile. They had gotten scruffy from the transformation. I closed my eyes and tried to get to my strange emotion, it was really hard this time. The strange emotion had caused me more pain than before, so much more that it was hard to transform back. *This is really difficult*, I thought. I focused on the thoughts I had before my discovery today. I could feel my joints loosening up, and the pressure of my blood running through my veins. Every strand of thick black hair stabbing back into my soft skin, even though it happened more quickly each time, I could start to feel where the pain was in each part of transformation.

I felt sick to my stomach knowing and thinking about how my beautiful enemy and twisted aunt had helped the hunters find me. If only I could decide when to transform, and not have to get tense. I got changed into my clothes and looked around, I could see Rob fishing in the lake acting extremely normally. Rob had a tendency of fitting into place as soon as he was outside in human form, he acted more carefully than in a panther form. Ben told me it's because he stayed in his animal form for too long. Rob lost the love of his life the night of his first change. Rob found it hard to look at me some days. Until I came along, the last woman he saw was Liana. He didn't realise his love, until that one day when he left and never came back.

I guess I have it easy some days but not today. 'Rob, Rob!' I shouted as I was running towards him. He just looked back at me in confusion. 'Get inside now!' I shouted as I was running I dived into the lake gliding through the cold, fresh water, 'til I got under the waterfall. I climbed up and waited on the edge for Rob, panicking as he should have been right behind. I gazed into the water just waiting; his face came towards me fast. Rob was amazing, he didn't climb out, he must have dived with such a force he jumped from the water.

'What's going on Chloe? I'm supposed to be on lookout while Brad is resting.'

'No one is going to be resting now ok? We have a big problem about to happen,' I couldn't help but take charge right now; I was not taking any chances.

I opened the door and stomped into the front room. Everyone at once stood up and Brad stumbled out of his pull-up bed. Ben looked at me in anger.

'Not now Ben please listen.' The horrid frown on his face dropped straight away. 'I've seen something in the forest today.' They all sat back down looking at me now with interest.

'Please carry on Chloe; we are all ears,' Adam said warmly. At that point I was in the middle of the room with all eyes on me.

'It was fast, white, and left a painful tension like it brands your memory.' At that point Ben and Adam's heads were in their cupped hands. 'The scent was like acid, burning away my face.' The boys then looked at each other in disgust. The thing I was describing was something they knew about.

The confusion must have been written on my face, as Adam stood up. Adam never stood up in group meetings. 'Ben will you and the others go and circle the perimeter? You know what to do.' Ben looked up at Adam and nodded.

'Chloe, you remember the new breeds?' Adam looked straight in my eyes.

'Yes,' I muttered in disgust, I screwed my face up tightly.

'They know where we are Chloe, we need to be prepared. It's only a matter of time. Chloe, just go with our precautions; their human form is blinding to our eyes.

They will look like any other human. But if you sense a track before they transform you can follow them.' The room was spinning out of control, my head full of facts that might have fitted together one day, but not that day.

I wanted a normal human life. A life where I could love and grow old naturally. A life worth living with the man I would love, who would not be my enemy who would protect me and respect me. My body and mind were longing for Charlie, just to see him and look into his eyes. I wanted him to be in my dreams for ever, I would wake up wishing they were real. But now my dreams were shattered into pieces, *but I know I will still be longing for him 'til my very last breath and heartbeat.* When my mind had relaxed I noticed Adam had gone, which meant I must as well. But I had no place to go.

I decided to take myself for a trip, it was the day I was supposed to be meeting Charlie. I'd had no sleep or rest, I closed my eyes and all I pictured was the bright red eyes and white fur of a new breed. *It's a nightmare I'm living.* I got myself out of the lake to the rocks. 'Chloe,' Tim shouted across. 'Where are you going? It's not safe.' I looked back over my shoulder.

'I'm going to a place where this mess does not exist anymore.' I couldn't help it but I needed time and space to overcome my fears.

'Why, Chloe? We need you here.' Tim's voice sounded uneasy and shaky.

'I will be more useful to you away,' I said as I turned my head and walked into the distance.

I felt my heart pounding and the heat rise through my bones. I didn't want to walk away; it was my home. I did not want to change either. I heard a roar; it had the presence of pain and sadness, I could tell by the tone it was Tim's. The noise was left ringing in my ears. I didn't know where I was heading, but I needed some human time to know who I was. I just wanted a last chance to live my life the way I should. I would then accept my fate and deal with it. If I survived, well then my heart would go on but the anger for what had happened to me would live forever.

Darker Than the Forest

I had been two months alone...

Things were not the same; Charlie was a distant memory. I'd been working in the town by the harbour in a small café, staying in the bed and breakfast above. Lying low hadn't been easy, I didn't want to be found or seen. Now and then people would look at me; I wasn't too kind to those who stared. I would heat up hotter in the café, a few times I been close to being fired. My employer was a kind man, he felt sorry for me. Frank called me "the girl with pain in her eyes".

Some days were hard; the pack was my family. And I was here, working on my target to be able to face my identity.

I went to the local bar every night without fail. Steak and chips with a bottle of wine, I had my own seat that I would reserve; I would wear a hat and contact lenses to hide my bright green eyes. I could hear the locals talk about me.

'The pretty girl over there what's her name?'

'I hear they call her a bottle of secrets that girl.'

All the hate and curiosity in the world wouldn't offend me, as long as they were human they couldn't do any harm to me.

I was settled now, I got up from my shabby room, with a sink to wash and a little window looking out to the harbour. I put on a black dress and heels, I popped my contacts in and headed downstairs. Life as a human wasn't all fun, I didn't miss the daily routines, the lonely nights and casual days.

'Morning Jenny,' I didn't use my real name it would have been too easy to be found.

'Morning Frank,' it was the busy time of year where fishing competitions were held, it made us very popular.

The cafe was full, my feet hurt for the first time in a while, running around in heels. It was the afternoon; I kept going through the day, full of energy. I was told I was Frank's best waitress as I never stopped, and worked double shifts. The takings were higher than ever before. There were lots of voices and people moving around by the counter. I noticed a scent; I couldn't remember whose scent. As I'd felt the black legend slip away from me each week I'd felt it draining me, and the instincts to transform were stronger, like the monster inside was ready to be free again. The black legend wanted me to change. I looked around the café, walking around, I was relaxed, not frightened. All of a sudden someone grabbed my hand; it was a firm grip. I didn't look round. There was a pause and my heart was beating fast.

'Sit down, Chloe,' he said. The voice was gentle. It startled me, *they found me,* I gasped. *My boy's found me;* I felt a smile spread across my face. I turned my head slowly; I couldn't believe my eyes, his name whispered through my lips.

'Charlie.'

Charlie's eyes looked at me, they had worry in them. I sat down. I didn't know what to say. He took my hands into his, they felt so warm.

'They need you Chloe; time is closing in on them. Your aunt is sending the hunters into your pack's direction; the new breed's leader is planning attack. They're outnumbered,' he said, he looked disappointed.

'How much time do we have?' I said, I felt my eyes welling up.

'Three weeks at the most, but you have some time to prepare.' Charlie knew all this information; I thought, *can he be trusted? Should I just take him out now? I'm so wary of him.* 'I know what you're thinking,' he said. I realised I was frowning.

'Sorry is it that obvious?' I asked. He looked down.

'I've been watching you for some time now, you've blossomed so beautifully. Your heart beat's grown stronger; your eyes brighten up the dark days. When I see you running through the forest, I miss a beat and it gets darker.' He stopped and looked up. He let go of my hands, sadness draped over his face.

'I was sent to finish you; a female panther was too risky to be left. When I didn't I became an outsider without a leader. Zak, the main hunter of this area, was tipped by a relative of his, I'm sorry to have to give you this unexpected news. Zak, his relative is your aunt; he also is your cousin.'

'Oh, oh, no! This is wrong. It can't be right. You're wrong.' I stood up and looked down, why couldn't he carry on with the nice compliments? 'Nice talking to you,' I walked towards the door.

'Hey Jenny,' Frank shouted. I still kept walking and slammed the door. I could hear Frank say. 'You tell that girl she's fired.'

As I was walking through the busy streets, trying to walk as fast as I could without being noticed, I was super quick on my feet. But before I had a chance he grabbed my shoulder and pulled me to an enclosed alleyway. We were inches away from each other, holding each other the way I dreamed in the forest. He stepped away.

'How can I trust you?' I said, looking into his eyes. I felt my heart pounding; I felt the fear again that made my tummy turn. He raised his hand and put it on my chest.

'I need you to trust me,' his voice slowed my beat; almost to the point I could feel my head go lighter. 'That's better.' Charlie then removed his hands from my chest. 'Let's walk,' he grabbed my hand and walked into the street, we headed towards the quiet part of the harbour where the competition was finishing. 'I wasn't stalking you Chloe, I couldn't do the task I was sent to do.' The weather was sunny and I was supposed to feel warm. 'They sent me because I was the strongest, they thought I wouldn't fall for the female legend,' he said like he was surprised with himself. I carried on listening carefully in case some information slipped out.

'But it happened. When you left I carried on watching the pack before I tracked you down. Your Ben is not coping well with your disappearance, they think you're dead,' *How can they think I'm dead? Are they too stupid to realise I am a lot more emotionally stable than most women? If Charlie was watching them and knew I was not dead, why did he not say anything to them?* 'I could not tell the boys, I would have been bitten to shreds with that many of them,' he said.

'Uh, how did you do that?' I stopped and looked up at him. He smiled, showing his perfect teeth. I was starting to remember all the feelings I felt before Ben told me he was a hunter.

We both sat on a bench looking out to sea. He pulled my face to look at him by my chin. 'I feel your feelings when we are close, I try not to feel it but you're so emotional,' he said, and I believed him. 'It was the day you changed and first laid eyes on me. It hit me so hard that I had to go fast.' I remembered that day at the doctors. 'You'd just been so angry, it made me angry.'

The only silly thing I could reply with was, 'Sorry.' I looked away.

'I want to help you,' he said.

'I don't need help,' I replied feistily.

'Yes you do, you lost your instincts, and how are you supposed to fight?' he said knowing full well how I was feeling. I wondered if words were more powerful than feelings.

'Excuse me if am aggressive and short tempered,' I said. He started laughing.

'Well, what your heart says differs,' he said.

'Oh, well, that's really funny, is it? Can't hide anything from you, great,' I said being dramatic. He didn't smile, I was now feeling sadness. I felt like I was absorbing his sadness, it was very unpleasant.

'Chloe I'm sorry, if you can understand you may see it's a burden or a death trap,' I could understand it was a burden, but why a death trap? *If feeling what I feel can kill you then love is deadly. Oh no, did I just say love in my head?*

'Death trap, that's a joke of yours?' I really needed help with this conclusion.

'It is Chloe, can't you see? We can't be apart, it's entirely my fault. If I didn't stay so close by you all this time, we wouldn't have connected and you would keep your own feelings and not share them with me,' he said it with painful sadness. His words made an impact on me, I realised we had been connected from the moment we met.

Charlie had always been on my mind; the thoughts had brought me great pleasure. 'I can't live without you,' he said. The sun was about to set in the harbour, it was very peaceful. I held his hand tightly.

'Then don't go,' I said like I meant every word and it came from the darkest part of my heart. I was waiting for his embrace just to see his emotions, not feel it inside. But he stood up and looked out to sea, he pulled me up by my hand.

'It's time we get moving,' Charlie's voice felt so cold.

'Where are we going?' I demanded.

'Back to the forest where you belong.' I didn't like the idea of the forest, I pictured it dark and evil. I pulled my hand free.

'You can think twice if you think I'm going back,' I felt so much anger, as if the thought had haunted me for weeks, of me ever going back.

'Yes you are, I don't need a second thought about this,' he said, frowning.

'And what are you going to do about it,' I said rationally.

He lost the frown and smiled, 'You can't pull that trick on me Chloe, I'm not that silly,' his words sounded belittling.

'So you're saying I'm a magician now? Pulling tricks on you?' I couldn't help but smile back.

'Huh, well I am just saying that if you think you're going to stop me because you're angry, well it won't work missy,' I realised at this point he was right; I had to go back.

How could I live with myself if I wasn't there and someone got hurt? I felt like I should not leave Charlie either, I was more myself around him. He made me feel human, just how I wanted. I felt light on my feet.

'You will be safe with me I promise I won't let anybody hurt you.' His eyes were trustworthy and his words strong enough for me to believe them. We walked along the harbour and up the main street near to the top of town. I picked up some items, the few clothes I had. Charlie picked up some food from the small stall.

As I went to let myself into his truck, he walked over to the passenger side to open the door for me. I didn't know if I should say thank you or that I could have done it myself. I looked at him and got in the truck. He drove out of the town up past Ella's house; I hadn't been there since the day we fell out. It seemed a long time ago now; she was safer without me being in her life. Friends would complicate things now.

I looked at Charlie and thought to myself; *is he my friend? Or possibly my feelings towards him show him I'm more?* I realised now that we were connected and our feelings connected as one. I felt scared of my emotions, especially when they were strong enough to change my form. *If he feels how I feel about him...* I wondered, *what if he feels the same?* We were still driving towards the outside of town towards the campsite. The rain was heavy, crashing down on the windscreen; we headed down a muddy track into the forest. The turning would have been difficult to find unless you knew it was there.

'This place, is it safe?' I said, feeling unsure of my safety. 'Do the other hunters know of this track?' I couldn't help but doubt my whereabouts.

'You will be safe here Chloe,' he said without expression on his perfect face. After travelling five miles down the track I could just about glance through the front window of his truck. There was a wooden cabin covered in ivy, with a porch for his truck. There was a little wooden door and window; the cabin looked like it was made from lots of different types of old wood. We pulled up under the porch; the rain was hitting the ground so hard. He let me out of the car. His t-shirt was drenched in rain water; it was dripping from his hair down his face. At that moment I could feel my heart race, I felt like the damsel in distress and he was my hero. 'Chloe, are you ok?' he said, still waiting for me to get out of the truck. He smiled at me; I forgot that he could feel my feelings towards him.

'Sorry,' I said as I jumped out the truck and lightly brushed past him. I ran fast to the front door of the cabin. He followed behind. Not even my sharp quickness stopped me from getting wet through.

As we walked into the cabin, I realised that in this one small room was a single size bed, and a corner chair with romance novels. Also I could see that to the far side was a fridge and a microwave. I stood shivering from the cold of my wet clothes, I couldn't remember the last time I felt cold, I used to never feel it. It was sad to know the power within me was still slipping away. He came up close to me with a long sweat shirt. 'Put this on,' he said to me but there was nowhere to get undressed.

I waited to see if he was going to leave the room, when Charlie, out of the blue, lifted his wet top off to change. I gasped as I couldn't believe my eyes. Underneath his clothing was a perfectly shaped, toned body. Every muscle had an outline, but I realised he was not going to put another top on. I couldn't complain at the view, and then suddenly caught on why he didn't. He knew I liked looking at him in this way. *I do, I think he likes the feeling he gets from me when I admire him.* I turned facing away from him and lifted my wet top off; my long hair covered most of my back. Before I put my top on I felt breathing on my neck, he gently moved my hair away and kissed my shoulder right up to my neck. He whispered in my ear, 'I just can't help myself when I'm near you.' I didn't want to say anything. My feelings could say more than words. I pulled his hand to my face and kissed his hand, he had very soft, gentle hands. He slowly moved his arms around my waist and pulled me closer to him. He rested his head on my shoulder, 'I could hold you forever,' Charlie said, looking out to the room.

'You can hold me like this forever,' I felt my heart skip, and butterflies.

I'd never been close to a guy who was not family. He slowly let go for me to get dressed. It was now night outside. I put on the long sweat shirt that covered me to my knees. I looked in confusion for where I would rest for the night. 'If it's ok with you, you may sleep in my bed tonight.' He started putting fresh sheets on the bed for me. I was looking at his collection of novels.

'Yes it will be fine thank you,' I said, yawning a little. I was getting very sleepy from the long day and hard discussions.

'Here,' he said. 'Your bed is ready for you, we've got a long day tomorrow,' Charlie said like he was excited to spend the day with me.

'Great,' I said standing up and climbing into the bed. Charlie kissed my forehead and walked over to the corner chair.

'There's room for one more, isn't there?' I asked. I felt guilty kicking him out of his own bed.

'Chloe,' he said in a strange tone of voice.

'Look I've had to share rooms and beds with my brothers in the pack; I think it won't upset me if you wanted to share,' Maybe it was the close company I wanted from Charlie, I'd been staying on my own for some time.

'If you say it doesn't upset you then, thanks,' he said as he stood up and walked over towards the bed. I turned over on my side to face the other side, close to the wall, so he didn't feel uneasy.

I was just drifting off to sleep and then I felt his arm come across my waist, Charlie snuggled himself right up close next to me. I felt relaxed and happy, I was not sure whether or not it was me feeling those emotions or if it was Charlie. I never thought I would end up feeling happy lying next to the person I cared most about. Not feeling used or hurt. It was because I trusted him enough to let him get close to me, let him in to see who I really was under my skin. It helped make me feel that it was all real and that he was not spinning a web of lies to get close to the enemy. I confused myself whether or not I was staying close to the enemy to find information, or did I want to spend time with him?

I missed Ben so much, and my brothers, especially Tim; his smile shined across every room he was in. I wondered to myself if Adam would forgive me for what I had done in leaving so long. And what I was doing now. I felt a sense of sadness and emotion across my chest, the sad thing was, I had no idea if these feelings were my own anymore, my feelings were too tightly linked to Charlie's. I kept pondering, as if I was trying to give myself an excuse not to be a part of what I'd become.

'Chloe,' Charlie called, 'you can't sleep?' I had no reason not to be sleeping and resting, but my instincts needed to be given into.

'I'm just going outside,' I replied.

'Stay close so I feel if you need me,' Charlie's concern was starting to become exasperating. But I couldn't help but fall for such caring and handsome charms.

I put my clothes back on, and stepped out onto the cabin porch. The air was fresh and cool, and the breeze felt gentle on my hair. I was on my own in complete darkness; I felt ready to feel fast and strong again and to hunt the wilderness. I wanted to get to that place so badly that I couldn't focus or even force a transformation like before. I was relaxed and calm too, for the first time in what seemed a decade. *When you want something it's harder to achieve*, I thought.

As I sat down with my legs crossed, I tried to find my inner emotions to bring up all that I had tried to forget. I closed my eyes, opening up my mind. All I saw was darkness, I tried harder and harder. I started to see my mum, beautiful and elegant in a black dress running through the meadow, her long dark bouncing hair with glistening golden specks. Then it all changed, in total darkness I saw her eyes looking evil with revenge, darkness filled her pupils. I had to carry on, I had no choice, I pictured my uncle lying dead on the floor half transformed with the person in the black hooded jacket standing over him with a knife. I had to stop my open mind visions, they were too haunting.

I could hear in the distance a light footstep just out of Charlie's perimeter, I didn't feel worried, if I was hurt or in danger I could sense all things to be afraid of. I could not smell a new breed or a hunter, just nothing. I wasn't afraid. I stood up and walked over toward the noise, it stopped. I pushed my head through the branches in the bush.

'Boo!'

I was spooked, I had never jumped or panicked so much in my life. It was Tim.

I couldn't find the words, so I grabbed hold of him and couldn't let him go. I pushed him behind the bush so Charlie wouldn't see him, or maybe so that Tim wouldn't discover Charlie.

'What are you doing here?' I asked Tim. We started walking into the forest.

'I had to find my Chloe,' Tim said looking at the surroundings. I felt guilt rushing around my body, it was suffocating me. 'The first few days you were gone were a piece of cake, but once a week passed, well it was not easy.' Tim had more of a manly stride, a husky musk scent. He seemed taller and darker; in fact, the more I looked at him the more I noticed his eyes were nearly black with specks of vibrant green. But it was definitely Tim, I could tell by his scent.

'Can I ask you something personal?' I asked him. There was a rock near the edge of a large embankment, I walked over towards the rock and sat myself by the edge. Tim followed with a look of confusion across his face. 'Why do you look so different? I mean you have totally changed. Your face shape, eyes, hair–' and that was when Tim cut me off

'Height?' he asked.

'So you realised yourself?'

'Course, Chloe! You must see us all now,' he said with excitement, 'our black legends have now awoken more than ever, it's awesome!' I sat in silence trying to read his signals, pick up on the differences in his personality. *It's still Tim.*

'Close your eyes and let your mind go dark.' He took my hand in his and pulled it closer to him, suddenly my mind was not so alone anymore, I felt a presence lingering. It was then, when I truly believed, that I saw two bright, green eyes in total darkness towering over me in my human form. I was trembling and terrified of these two huge eyes looking down at me. I could see trees, lots of trees and marshy terrain. The beast's two canine teeth were as big as my index finger, points so sharp they could pierce through bones. Its legs must have finished by my shoulders; the thought of what I could see was amazing yet terrifying. It couldn't be impossible. I quickly pulled my hand back towards myself; I looked at Tim with such confusion.

'It's... It's impossible.'

'It is not. Adam was shocked himself. He is the oldest and first in many decades to transform. It's part of us, were born like this,' Tim sounded so relaxed and calm but I did not wish to believe this monster was my potential.

'How did this happen?' I demanded.

'We were all not fully developed, it's an amazing theory. Adam was looking at old documents from our ancestors; here I brought it with me. Your eyes only Chloe.'

I looked down to the fragile stained paper it felt almost like cloth. And began to read:

The night was young upon a fine evening; the sky was a clear opening to our ancestors. Brothers meeting and pleasant companions served my legends meeting under a natural form of light, from the sky and surrounded around a warming flame from fire. It was this night our mind joined together to form the bond that was waiting deep within our souls. The bond is the beginning. And the end to our many long years of waiting, hunting, and training, it was the beginning of the new black legends pack. The pack chief knows when his calling is; to begin a group of guards stronger and harder, we are now bigger and appearance changes may alter due to the ages of the fellow men and I. The bond may seem complete and at its full strength but sadly this new group is missing the key. Rumours have been noticed which say that the key is

*within a woman whom is special and delightful, with
beauty and pure elegance and respect. Though deep in her
mind is a place that is full of energy and sparks so they
say. A mind that is powerful but still misleading. She is
destined for love, more power, her brothers will face fear
in their hearts. She will be driven to a force, then is too
late. If thou ever finds the powerful lady she will sit next
to the chief leader, and she will blossom too, into the pack.
Always believe within her soul; beware of her existence
as she will always choose love and peace.*

It was inspiring 'til the point I realised the letter
sounded like it was describing me. Not the complimenting
or the elegance, because women were different in those
days, it was the peace of mind. I couldn't help but try to
pretend I was still reading so I could think of what to say.

'We need you back,' he said, sad and hopeful.

'I can't, not yet,' How was I able to become stronger,
when I'd become weak as my human self? Tim must not
know that I'd chosen love. I would lose everything; I was
a changed individual. Love had become a big part of who
I was, I'd come back because of it. I felt it. But I didn't
know why I loved so much and felt butterflies in my
stomach. I looked at Tim and how warm he looked; he
had gentle eyes and smooth skin. His scent was fresh and
musky. Seeing him like this, made me see Tim in a
different light.

'Chloe,' I heard my name as I realised I was gazing
into Tim's eyes, I didn't even realise how my head had
turned to his direction. For the first time I blushed; I felt
stupid as this guy had seen me without clothes on so many
times. 'Chloe,' he laughed and smiled.

'Sorry,' I said, looking away. He put his arm around me, I look back into his eyes.

'You seem different girl, Ben won't approve of this,' he smiled again. *This is wrong I cannot feel like this how can I fancy Tim? I mean Tim has always been nice and pleasant to look at, but wow that smile can make your heart skip a beat!*

'He will never approve of my choices in life,' I stood up to get back before sunrise.

'Ben needs you and I do too, I miss having a girl about to calm down the male egos.' I looked at him; my face must have had sorrow written across it. His smile faded away.

I turned my back and ran into the distance. *I don't know what just happened, feeling warm and fuzzy for a few moments. This is not meant to be this way; Charlie is who I need to concentrate on. We have some kind of spiritual connection I guess. Plus, there is only one of me, what am I thinking? Tim?!* I laughed to myself. The most idiotic thing of all was that I didn't even know how I felt about either of them and their feelings for me. Obviously, I knew Charlie did have feelings for me, but Tim was mysterious and like family. As I walked to clear my thoughts it still played on my mind, *Tim wow, Tim wow.* I had no idea why I kept saying his name; I guessed that fuzzy feeling was nice. The blood in my cheeks finally let go and my blush began to fade.

I had just arrived outside the cabin. 'It's time,' Charlie said standing outside with his arms crossed.

'I'm ready.'

When love goes down it is a strange sensation, being ready and wanting something so badly. I looked at Charlie thinking, *he'll do anything for me, he is safe,* he was mysterious but at the same time I felt passionate towards him.

I felt my mind was not in the same field, *I should concentrate on fighting rather than loving and letting my heart sink for the wrong reasons.* 'Chloe are you ready?' Charlie said, looking at me as I stared into space.

'Sorry,' I felt like such a dummy sometimes. I closed my eyes tightly, trying to get into the right frame of mind, but I didn't feel right. I felt nothing.

'Chloe what's taking so long?' I ignored him. I felt Charlie was being a typical man edging me on and I couldn't handle it.

'Can you give me some more space please?' I snapped.

'Ok fine in your own time,' I felt I was being pushed into something that did not feel natural anymore. I didn't think of Charlie, I tried not to. Without wanting to I thought of Tim, I realised we had a connection that could not be understood. But I felt drawn to loving Charlie, desperate for him to be caring and holding on to me.

Charlie stood looking at me, his amazing eyes checking every part of my body. I noticed how he held himself. It was at this moment I knew he was more to me than I had ever realised. I couldn't control myself anymore. I couldn't resist his scent and the fact that I was not running my fingers through his hair. I wanted to hold him with my hand on his face. Without thinking I ran to him, he didn't flinch, he stayed very still. I got closer to him, my head told me not to, but my heart told me otherwise. I latched my lips upon his, I felt like sparks were flying. The intensity ran deep.

He didn't try to push me away, Charlie held me by my waist. I ran my hands through his hair. As I pulled away and looked up into his eyes, I wanted this moment never to end. The forest seemed brighter and fresher, I knew I was ready. *I know what I am fighting for.* But my fight was now on a completely new level. 'Don't ever leave my sight again,' Charlie smoothly said as he stroked my face. 'I could not go another day without seeing such beauty,' he said. The guy in my dreams said, such amazingly lovely words.

'The day you will never see me again is the day I'm dead, I promise,' I replied, really wanting to say something a little more special but who was I kidding? I was not good at romance.

'I don't want to think of you dead right now Chloe,' he grinned.

I didn't know what to say. I kissed Charlie again hoping that my kiss would explain. I couldn't work out in the heat of the moment what was really going on but I was ready. I pushed him away and smiled.

'Catch me if you can,' I ran as fast as I could, I felt as quick as I did before, maybe even faster. I could hear Charlie's footsteps behind me; he was quick and gaining fast. I leapt into the air as I was still running and without thought I changed, and even with the pain and burning sensation it was great. I could hear Charlie laughing.

'Nice try, cheat,' he shouted. I wanted to reply and say "it's practice", I loved bantering with him.

We had been running for at least seven miles, I was ecstatic! Being back on four legs took me back; I had forgotten how much fun it used to be. *Things have changed. Charlie is right it is time to go back.* Charlie was behind me; he was keeping up with me the whole time and sometimes in front. I'd really missed the feeling of freedom. I just wanted to go back to the pack. But I couldn't, I'd miss Charlie. I stopped running and turned back, it took miles of running to get my clothes. Charlie was gazing at my body, looking in frustration.

'Like what you see?' I said, jokingly. Charlie turned round to look the other way. I walked up behind him and placed my hands on his shoulder and kissed his neck gently. He grabbed my hand.

'Stop,' he said.

'What if I don't want to?' without a warning, in a snap he turned to me and pushed me up against a tree.

'I want you as much as you want me, and nothing can stop the chemistry. But at least we can control it,' I looked deep into his eyes trying to work out why.

'If you want me you can have me, what does control have to do with something that feels so natural? So right,' It was hard to believe that I was having a talk about chemistry and control whilst stood completely bare in front of Charlie.

'It means everything Chloe, damn right everything, open your eyes,' he said.

'My eyes are open, looking into the eyes of someone who don't realise how much trouble I could be in just by looking at them,' I replied sternly; it seemed like he didn't realise what a risk I had taken, being with him. I'd left my pack for a long time. I should have been with my own.

'Chloe I know, sorry for my reckless behaviour, I do want you and understand how you feel, and I feel it too remember.' I picked my clothes up and started to dress myself.

'I have to go back, it been too long,' I said in a lower, sad tone. Looking around at the beautiful sight of the forest, I looked back at Charlie. His face was full of disappointment I could feel it too, the magnetic force that was fixing us together. With not a thought or a word to discuss the situation, I turned and walked away into the darkness of the trees. I had been such a long time away from my pack I had lost track of my roots. At each step I took away from Charlie, I felt numb, incomplete.

I could still feel Charlie and smell his scent as I continued to find the lake; part of me wasn't angry that he was following me. Knowing how much he cared hurt, I could not take him with me nor could he be seen either but I'd been worried since Charlie spoke of Zak, goose-bumps covered me at the very thought of him. I often wondered, if push came to shove, would Charlie be by my side if the hunters came for me? I knew I had the pack but recently I'd not had their back.

The forest was quiet as morning had awoken, *it's too quiet*. You could normally hear the birds singing and flying, I looked around, above into the trees, and the sky became red. Feeling sick with nerves wasn't something I'd grown accustomed to. I could start to smell musk and it was familiar, I was at the edge of the lake. I pushed myself through the ferns, being cautious before I appeared. In front of me I could see Ben, Adam, Brad, Rob, and Tim. All with their arms crossed looking unimpressed to see me, apart from Tim of course. The awkward silence was terrifying; *have I been shut out from the pack?* Adam gave me a nod and walked towards my direction, the others walked away towards the waterfall.

'Come,' he said to me, and I started to follow a good few steps behind. 'Are you better?' Adam asked.

'Yes,' I said trying not to reveal too much information that could be used against me.

'Good, because if you leave us again you will not return,' Adam sounded serious, he wasn't taking any prisoners.

'I will be the best I can be,' I replied, and he nodded once. Not one single smile or expression cracked his face and I knew I'd done wrong.

We reached the waterfall and the others had already jumped into the water. I knew that as soon as I got into the water there wasn't any turning back. I inhaled a deep breath and turned to look back; Charlie was watching in the distance; I took one good long look and smiled. I felt like I was straining against the magnetic force between us. Before I could even begin to think about going back to him, I jumped into the lake. The lake partially felt like home, it'd been so long since I was last feeling comfortable, facing the pack, together like we used to.

Climbing out behind the waterfall I saw Tim waiting to help me up, trying to be a gentleman. Knowing full well I could do it by myself, I smiled.

'Thank you,' he said. I didn't need to ask why he was thanking me, I could tell he was just grateful I had returned.

The room was quiet; Adam was sitting in his chair while Rob was looking through books. I looked around to find Ben and he wasn't there; confused, I walked around the corner to the bunk room. He was just sitting with his head in hands, Ben also looked bigger and taller than when we had last spoken.

'Hi,' I said, quietly, trying not to startle him.

'Nice for you to show your face,' Ben said sadly.

'I know I haven't been around when you all needed me the most, but I would have been no use to any of you. My mind was confused and my soul was hurting, I would only have kept you all back.' My words were truthful but I still felt I was lying, because I had enjoyed being away and having freedom.

'It's not that,' Ben replied. 'I failed you! I was irrational, telling you things that should be told with great care. I don't know how to handle actual blood related family.' Ben had a point, he had been away from family for many years! His mum was a traitor and he had lost his father because of it. *Nothing I can do could be worse than what she has done; or could it?* I thought. *Charlie is one of them, that's the trouble; am I just like Aunt Jane?*

'Do you know who Zak is?' I asked Ben.

'Zak! What about Zak?' Ben looked shocked that I mentioned his name.

'How Is Zak your cousin?' I asked, knowing now might not be the best time to ask such things.

'He's my Uncle Derek's son, I've met him and Zak only a few times, when Zak was young. Mum used to tell me he lives in South America and couldn't afford to see us often. I actually believed my mother for years! How stupid am I?'

Ben sounded disappointed with himself, I couldn't say I blamed him.

'Do you know he isn't in South America anymore?' I replied. Ben didn't seem surprise by my information.

'Zak is with my mum I gather?' he asked.

'Yes, he has been the one tracking me down, it seems they are only interested in finding me,' I looked to the floor.

'Who told you? I mean how do you know so much?' he asked.

I couldn't say Charlie told me, nor could I say a hunter had been looking out for me. 'I've been watching from a distance and I gather it was him,' lying was not really my forte, especially to Ben. 'They are after me because they are worried about my potential, and I gather they also think I'm a threat,' I was not sure how to smooth this over, to not sound so scary.

'We must tell the others.'

A week passed and snow started to fall, the water became very icy outside the cave, so we were stuck indoors. Lots of discussions and preparations had been going on. Rob found more ancient documents that discussed the ritual that proved female legends did exist, although we already knew that of course. Adam wanted to perform the ritual but we couldn't get out the cave, he also predicted once the snow had melted we could expect visitors. 'They know we are weaker when winter comes. It's the perfect time to attack!'

I thought he was right but we couldn't sit and wait around, and waste time hoping that we could fight, hoping we could get the ritual done before we were all done for!

Someone would have to go and check outside or find another way.

'This sucks,' Brad broke the silence. 'Surely ice can't hurt us, we are capable with dealing with the cold,' he continued.

'There is cold water, Brad, and then there is ice water, idiot,' Rob replied, tension filled the room.

'I'm no idiot, we can't sit and wait can we stupid,' Brad bit back. Before we knew it, we were sat watching Brad and Rob scrap like children, making a racket and knocking things over.

'Enough,' Adam shouted looking very cross. 'We may be animals but we don't always have to act like them,' he yelled. With that the boys stopped and stood up and nodded at Adam.

When you nodded at the pack leader you were showing respect, it took me a little while to figure this out previously. 'If any of you have a better idea of getting out without suicide, then speak up,' Adam looked around, waiting.

'We dig our way out.' Ben stood up. 'We have claws, and besides, to the back of the cave there is soft earth,' Ben sounded hopeful.

One thing Ben didn't think of was how we would keep this a secure hiding place with two exits.

'It's worth a try,' Rob replied.

'If we don't try we will just have minimised our chances,' Tim spoke up. He sat quietly waiting for Adam's approval, rubbing his chin thinking about the possibilities.

'Ok,' Adam said.

Ben smiled as it was his idea that had been approved, and Rob was normally the one with bright ideas.

The guys lit up the back of the cave with oil lamps and looked carefully, deciding where to dig; in order to make this work we had to all do our bit. The cave wasn't big enough for us to put the left-over dirt out of the way and we would have to use the bunk room, which meant we would all have to sleep in the main cave. It made me wonder how they created such a home in the first place. The main area was all wood flooring and the wooden walls were like a cabin's almost.

Ben took the first shift to dig while Brad phased, and used large paws to scoop the dirt away. Watching someone phase so easily was very strange to me, my strange emotions gave me motive when phasing, *I wonder what Ben's motive is.*

It took three days of hard work and dedication to make a tunnel; some of the wood from the walls was ripped down and used to stabilise the new tunnel. We didn't know how far we had to go to get out, but Ben predicted that by tomorrow we would see daylight. *The fresh air will feel like bliss on my skin, and to hear the breeze through the trees.* Suddenly I thought of Charlie, and how I hadn't seen him for days maybe weeks, it felt like forever in the cave. We hadn't had a chance to keep track of time. Imagining Charlie, and him being alone watching over us, made me feel sad, even though he was more than capable of looking after himself. Words could not describe how much I missed his face and smelling his intoxicating scent.

Since being back with the pack my instincts were returning to me, I felt a part of two worlds again. This time I was not so afraid. I'd had chances to talk to each member when it was not their turn to dig, and they'd been helpful and understanding; one thing I still didn't know much about was the new breeds, I felt Rob would be the best person to talk to; he was a little book-worm most of the time.

I knew more about the hunters than they realised, in some of the discussions with the pack I'd had to pretend what they told me was all new news, about how some hunters could run really fast and how they could be very similar to humans, the only difference was how super strong they were.

All I knew of the new breeds, was how they smelt terrible, and how it burned like acid to smell them, and that they didn't like us, not a huge amount of information to go by in all fairness. *I mean how am I supposed to fight them when, I'm not completely sure what we are fighting for. I'm not sure anymore what is darker than the forest.*

We were all resting after a hard shift of digging, Ben and Brad had already fallen asleep and Rob was once again reading a book, while Adam was still trying to work out the ritual. Tim was sitting next to me and put his hand out for me to touch, so I touched his hand with a friendly gesture. He whispered, 'Close your eyes.' I closed them and then pictured darkness. I felt Tim enter my mind.

I saw a winter wonderland, lots of snow swirling around us, we were walking along a track in the forest; there was white everywhere, with icicles hanging off some trees. It was beautiful, the sky was clear, not a bird in sight. I felt a thud on my back, I turned to see Tim with a snow ball ready to throw again, laughing I chased him, picking up snow on the way. Tim hid in the trees and it almost became like a game of paintball but with snow, I could feel a smile growing on my face and saw Tim smile back. I felt his hand let go and darkness filled my mind again.

'That was fun,' I said as I open my eyes again. 'It's a shame we are stuck indoors,' I continued as he looked, smiling at me.

'When did you realise you can show people your vision through touch?' I asked him.

'I've have always been able to, it's a gift, isn't it?' he said.

'Yeah, a really cool gift if you don't mind me saying,' I replied.

I looked around the room thinking, and I wondered if anyone else had a gift, something unique about them. I looked at Ben and Brad, they had always been very basic and I hadn't noticed any peculiar habits of theirs yet. While Rob, on the one hand, was very clever, I did feel he was more than just a messenger, being Adam's right hand man. Tim, however, I guess he had always been a bit more special, more gentle and caring. He never seemed to mind if he was asked for anything, now and then he still worked in the campsite to provide us with supplies.

I hadn't been back to the campsite; I had completely forgotten. I just left without a thought; Tim did tell me that I had lost my job and that someone else had taken over. To be honest I didn't care, I had more important things happening in my life. I started to yawn and curled up with my head on Tim's lap, he started stroking my hair and gave me a friendly kiss on my head. 'Sleep well Chloe,' he whispered.

The Fear That Melts

I woke up with a pillow under my head, the room was quiet. No one was in sight, in such a small place there was always someone in the room; unless they had completed the tunnel. I stirred, moving slowly as I began to stretch.

'Ah good you're awake,' Tim said as he popped his head into the room.

'Where is everyone?' I wondered.

'Outside,' he replied.

I got to my feet and gave him a nod and followed Tim towards the new tunnel. It was very dark and smelled very damp.

We had been a while walking in complete darkness, but we could see very well. The tunnel was longer than I thought and I could see now why it took so long. I started to see a bright light ahead and a narrow exit with bushes covering over. I gently pushed myself through and could see the others wandering around. It looked as if they had found something.

'Guys, over here!' Adam shouted from a distance, he was by the lake's perimeter. Tim and I ran over towards him. Looking down we could see footprints; we couldn't work out if they were hunters' or hikers'. 'Hikers don't come down this far,' Adam said looking concerned. I crouched down closer and took in the scent. *It's Charlie's! Oh no!*

'Could be hunters? They've been tracking us for a while now, maybe Chloe returning has given them the scent they are looking for,' Rob said.

'These tracks are old, the scent is nearly non-existent,' I said trying to drive their attention away. But I had a feeling this wasn't going to be let go of.

'I'll try and have a sniff. I've smelt hunters before, once, it might bring a memory back,' Rob continued.

'No!' I shouted, they all turned and looked at me. 'I mean I've already tested and it's fine, I would remember the scent if I'd smelt it at Aunt Jane's, wouldn't I?'

They turned and looked back at the print, 'I hope you're right Chloe, besides we have a lot to do.'

Brad continued on to his normal lookout spot and Rob went to Adam's side. Ben was up in the tree, tracking down a meal in his other form. Ben loved catching birds to eat, the others mostly liked game. I still hadn't got to grips with hunting my own food; I shared Ben's meals most of the time. Tim used to go and get me things when I visited before I left, he used to get told off by Adam, saying that I should get my own. Adam wanted me to be just like the others, smart and fast and always using my animal instincts not my human ones.

Then we all began to hunt. One by one they phased, running off in the snow, it always amused me seeing the clothes looking like they just puffed off, like a spell. I was the last to phase to go on the hunt to find my meal, I didn't enjoy it very much. I started running fast and, like a kettle boiled to breaking point, I gave in to my strange emotions. Feeling for that one moment that could only be explained in slow motion, waiting for the feel of muscle tearing under the skin, my nose pushing and pulling, teeth stretching through my gums which always felt sore. Hair piercing through my soft skin. All my bones popping out of joint as the repositioning took place. Although this sounded like a lot, it honestly only took two seconds. The first phase would always be the most painful experience I'd ever had; it was the longest transformation, the first. The others explained theirs to me once, most of them also blacked out the first few times.

I'd split off from the others, and continued to hunt more in the south of the forest. Sniffing the area step by step, I slowed myself down, not one murmur. *Ah... that smell it's so intoxicating,* I knew it was Charlie. I couldn't phase back in such a short time without bringing something back for the others, they'd ask questions if I returned without food. I stood still, waiting. I felt happy, I could feel it was not just me feeling it too. His face appeared, looking wary, I wondered if he knew for sure it was me.

He cracked a big smile and I felt warm inside, if only I could phase back and talk to him.

'You survived! I know you can't talk back to me, but I've been worried while you were trapped,' he said without whispering. I began to worry that the others would find us; I rubbed my head against his hand and left, for his safety. I could feel sadness again, and this time I knew it was from him, because I was feeling more scared than anything. I wanted to stay with him, hug him with my arms, touch his face. He looked over as I carried on, putting distance between us. *That was close,* I thought to myself. *I can't believe Charlie would take such a risk. It's so good to see him though, still as handsome as ever.*

I heard a loud "SNAP" to my left; I could smell the deer about one hundred feet to my left. My adrenaline started to shake through me, as my mouth began watering from hunger. I tried to be stealthy like a real human hunter, making my way slowly, going through the ferns. I saw the deer up ahead; I began to move forward, this time treading lightly. The silence in the air made this harder; my heart was pounding in desperation. I was close, though, to making my move, ready to pounce, I counted down. *One, two, three, four,* 'What the...?' I said to myself. Before I could count to five Ben had beaten me to the hunt and had pounced and killed the dear in a quick flash. I looked at him in anger, I was so close to finally proving that I had what it took and Ben swooped in and took the opportunity away!

It was getting close to nightfall; the pack had been out hunting for a good amount of time and once again I'd come back empty handed.

I phased back to my human form where I left my clothes. Adam didn't look impressed with me. Ben was laughing in the background with a large grin on his face, walking toward me. 'Don't worry Chloe we can share, like always,' Ben bragged as he walked on with a large deer over his shoulder.

Something looked different by the new cave entrance; Adam had been busy by the looks of it. Logs were placed in a circular position with fire wood in the middle. Adam sat down and took out a book from his pocket. I felt something light and fluffy touch my bare skin, looking up I saw huge fluffy snowflakes coming to land smoothly on the ground. Sometimes I forgot what time of year it was, being out of civilisation.

We all began to walk over to see what the deal was with Adam and his book.

'It's time,' Adam said, looking at his book as we approached with our arms crossed. We stood in silence waiting for Adam to explain what it was time for and why there was such a set up outside the hidden cave which no longer looked hidden. 'The ritual, that I had discovered before isn't the actual one, it was a hoax used many years ago to make villagers believe in the black legends' strength. But the truth is, there is a ritual I have found, and it's slightly more dangerous,' Adam paused.

Dangerous? How dangerous, I wondered, *more danger isn't something I like the sound of.*

'The female has to sacrifice herself to the spirit world, and Chloe before you jump to any conclusions the sacrifice is a token of your blood, the spirits might take more than you offer but never your life.'

'This sounds too risky Adam,' Ben said shaking his head.

'Is it really necessary?' Tim questioned.

'It's necessary if you want to be able to have a fighting chance with the enemy,' Adam said sternly.

'Then when?' I said sharply, if this had to be done then why argue? I was the one that was most likely going to get hurt.

'Tonight,' Adam stood up and walked into the tunnel. We all looked at each other with worried eyes, waiting for the silence to break.

'I'm fine honestly, I'll have a better night's sleep if I know I can kick ass,' I mentioned.

'Ha ha! Kick ass! You Brits say it so posh,' Brad joked. I gave him a punch in the arm and he didn't even flinch. I felt we were already made of strong steel, but I somewhat imagined we could be more powerful if we tried this. I touched Tim and showed him my thought, I showed him us, big and beautiful and fierce and strong.

'I hope so,' he whispered.

'Me too,' I said, looking hopefully into his eyes.

'You can show thoughts too,' he said, surprised, and held my hand, gently putting a reassuring amount of pressure into his grip.

The word sacrifice played on my mind, I always linked sacrifice to death and darkness. *You see spiritual and mythology movies with graphic deaths, pleading to the gods to give them what they want or need. Never ends well if I remember, the sacrifice gets away or slaughtered to the gods. Either way I won't be dying tonight,* I thought, taking one last breath. But I had a gut feeling and it was telling me this could either be the end, or a new beginning.

Every day since I had discovered I could transform, I had felt the fear melting away my emotions. It made it hard to understand and process all of the events from this year.

The cave was filled with light as I entered, the pack was sitting eating their prey. Ben gave me a wink and the others continued to enjoy their meals. Finding space between Rob and Ben I grabbed what was left of the deer, even though this deer was my prey that I lost it was still just as satisfying. Adam hadn't eaten much which was strange as he was the fastest eater I knew. He was still holding and reading the ritual book, studying the pages one by one, thoroughly. This made me more nervous, danger crossed my mind again. Adam wiped his forehead as he was perspiring, which I could only imagine was from the pressure of leading during a situation like this. Looking around the room I saw the others were peaceful and too quiet for my liking. *Where is the play fighting? Why aren't Rob and Brad arguing about who is right and who is wrong? Why isn't Ben next to Adam asking loads of questions?* I thought.

The peace continued for an hour, which felt more like three! Adam finally closed the book, slowly looking up. He looked directly at me, 'How are you feeling Chloe?' he asked.

'Strange,' I said without effort.

'Good, strange is good,' he smiled. We didn't often see Adam smile but when he did it was a little creepy. He stood up, nice and tall, and looked down.

'As your pack leader I command you to go outside and sit in a circle, you will hold hands willingly and you will remain quiet unless I ask you to do differently. You will not smile and whatever happens in the circle you will stay seated and not move an inch.'

I could hear myself swallow hard, *this sounds serious*. My heart began to pound in fear, I felt like human Chloe, scared from her first day at school, and the headmaster was Adam.

Following the pack, leaving the cave, doing what we were told, *why so official? What is the ritual?* I wondered. It was dark outside as I found a space round the circle of logs; the circle wasn't very big at all. I took my place next to Brad and Tim; Adam was lighting a fire. The night was clear with the stars sparkling in the darkness, no wind or breeze, just cold and white from the snow. *It doesn't matter how hot blooded we are, this feels cold.*

Adam sat down holding Ben's hand and Ben then held Brad's hand then Brad held mine, I looked at Tim as I went to hold his and I saw fear and regret shining in his eyes. Once holding his hand, I showed him strength, which of course meant I was showing Brad too. Tim then held Rob's hand and then the strangest most wonderful feeling happened when Rob held Adam's hand. It was like being in another person's skin but not just somebody, everybody in our circle; I could get in their heads. Closing my eyes, I saw someone's mind, it looked like they were thinking of food, so possibly Brad's. Oh and someone picturing a warm bath and books, *ah that must be Rob*. I then saw Aunt Jane with a dark expression on her face, enhancing her aged skin, *Ben! That must be Ben.*

'Today we come, asking for the help of our ancestors, the great and the powerful, to fulfil our needs and to keep the existence of our kind. War is coming and we are too weak to fight alone,' Adam said with his eyes closed and head upward.

This was very strange and weird, very creepy and somewhat awkward.

'We have two true bloodlines in our pack, one male and a female. We would like to offer her blood as a token of respect and the truth of her bloodline, with his token we want what is rightfully ours in return. To realise our potential, to protect the people we care about, and to change the fate of the pack,' Adam ended and we sat in silence.

'Come to the Fire Chloe, let go and grab the blade in front of you.' The blade was nothing I had ever seen before, sculpted dark wood with the design of our kind engraved on it; the blade was long and shiny, possibly very sharp. I was not sure what I was supposed to do with this blade, I looked to Adam for guidance.

'Blood is blood, from head to toe, take from wherever you can bestow.' Adam was still talking with his eyes shut. I looked around the circle at my brothers. I saw the burning flames in their eyes, the fears which I didn't often see. I brought the blade up and thought about where to bleed. I looked to my other hand and quickly, without thought, I sliced my hand deep enough to bring blood. At first it didn't hurt, but after two seconds it stung as the blood started pouring from my fresh wound. I placed my hand over the fire and let it fall freely, I felt weak and light headed, and cold, very cold. My head hurt and the pain felt excruciating.

I fell onto my knees close to the small fire, blood draining from my hand. Heartbeat slowing, as darkness filled my vision. All that was left for me to vaguely see was Adam's serious face through the fire, my very last thought was, *what has he done to me?* And I was gone.

Unexpected Visit

I woke up gasping for air, eyes still closed and mouth so dry. Slowly I opened my eyes; I was lying in the cave with Tim by my side. *What has happened?* I wondered, 'Agh!' I shouted as I sat up fast.

'Chloe, it's ok,' Tim reassured me, but I didn't care about him reassuring me.

Looking at my hand I saw no scar from the ritual, I tried touching it and pressing where the wound was, and still no pain. Something inside me still didn't seem the same; I was not worried nor was I happy to be alive. When Tim was by my side I normally felt happy, but I felt nothing.

'How long have I been out for?' I asked Tim. He looked at me strangely.

'You've been out cold; all of last night and all morning,' Tim replied.

'And the others, where are they?' I asked, *something really doesn't feel right, I can't feel at all.*

'They are out on the lookout,' Tim said, still looking at me in confusion.

'What is your problem?' I snapped.

'I'm confused,' said Tim. 'See the ritual worked; we have grown in strength and our muscles are bigger, and we are taller. But you–' he stuttered.

'What?' I snapped again.

'Your eyes! They're so green. Well they were green before but now they are brighter than ever. How are you feeling?' he asked.

'Nothing, I feel absolutely nothing. Like a hole is in my chest. It feels like every breath I take has no reason, no passion, no sadness, I feel no love in my heart.'

'You've just woken up, give it time,' he replied.

'I need air or something, maybe you're right.' Sitting on the edge I put my old, tired shoes on and pulled a black hoodie on, the one Tim got for all of us.

As I entered into the open air, taking a deep breath, there was still nothing. Looking around I saw the set-up from yesterday evening and ash on the floor. The others were no place to be seen.

Walking in the opposite direction from the lake I took nice, long strides, looking at the sun shining through the trees making the snow glisten. *It doesn't seem cold at all, strange,* I thought. Looking down at my hand again there was still not one scratch or cut, even in the day light. *Hmm odd, so it looks like the ritual has worked and I'm healing fast,* I was more alive than ever but not in the sense of happiness. My shoes felt tight and my old jeans even tighter I felt bulkier, more stable, but this didn't concern me, it gave me confidence.

As I continued my walk, further away from the lake, on my own, making sense of my body, I noticed a scent; one that wasn't pleasant; my nose twitched and my eyes felt slightly watery. *It's them, with the acid effect up my nose, it has to be.* I would have normally hid and stayed still or gone the other way from danger, but my feet continued to move down the natural path I often took, I was not scared.

I saw a young man with pure, white-blonde hair, as I got closer I noticed his piercing blue eyes. He was tall and slim with the biggest smirk on his face. His cheek bones stood out and his skin was pale.

'So we finally meet,' he said cockily, eyes staring at mine. I walked closer to him and he stood his ground. I got closer and his smirk started to fade. The closer I got the more rage I felt.

I grabbed him by the neck with one hand and lifted him into the air and then against the tree, 'Why are you here?' I asked with anger in my voice.

He didn't answer so I gripped his neck more firmly; he let out a slight groan and laughed in my face. He made me rage even more, in fact I had no idea what I was capable of. He must have been ten stone or more and I lifted him up with one hand, it was impossible but I was still able to continue. I let him down. '

'That was an easy interrogation, I didn't tell you what you want, but still you let me go,' he smirked.

'Tell me what I want and I won't interrogate you again, promise,' I knew deep down I wouldn't keep the promise. He looked blankly at me again, moving his head to one side. 'Who are you?' I shouted at him again.

He smiled, 'That's better, I like to be introduced before I get down to business.' He put his head straight and narrowed his eyes. There was something very odd about his behaviour, like he was trying to play a game. 'William is my name,' he said sounding very formal. He had very informal body language almost awkward looking, but his voice sounded, not British, but well spoken.

'William I ask you again, why are you here?' I stood, feet apart, hands on both hips, with my head held high and my hair moving in the cool breeze.

'And you are?' he asked. He was really testing my patience with this stupid game he was trying to play. I quickly, in one swift motion, grabbed William's arm and twisted it behind his back, pushing him to the ground so he was lying face down. I put my foot on his back and held him to the ground.

He shouted in pain and continued to laugh afterwards. 'You're a very brave woman, you can try and force the information out of me but I will give it freely if you tell me your,' I pulled his arm tighter, 'name!' He shouted and continued to laugh again.

I'd managed to suss out William, he was a messenger. A clever but stupid messenger who could have saved himself a lot of pain. But I had no remorse for his kind and pushed my foot down firmer on his back; I was just about to dislocate his shoulder.

'Chloe,' Adam shouted, 'stop!' He shouted again and the pack ran towards us. 'Let him go,' Adam ordered, when he shouted orders it used to niggle me but now it just hacked me off!

I dropped William's arm down from his back and grabbed the other arm, pulling him up and restraining him. 'That's not letting him go Chloe,' Adam said with an expression I could only explain as the look a teacher gives when you're misbehaving but they can't punish you.

But I was not letting him go. *We don't know why he is here, and where the others are.* William turned his head and whispered in my ear, 'Nice to meet you Chloe.'

I felt a shiver down my spine at how creepy he was, and held his wrists tighter.

'Your name, sir?' Adam asked.

The air was quiet and then finally, 'William, I am a messenger for the new more superior breed,' he grinned.

'Not anymore,' Brad piped up, but Adam's look soon brought Brad back down.

'Well as I am here I might as well share the good news, we know where you all are now and will be very happy to pay a visit,' William said very sarcastically. I twisted his wrist and he let out a small scream and then started laughing again.

'Come for us William, be our guests, but we are not your enemy,' Adam said, walking closer to William.

'How do you figure that out? We've been natural enemies for hundreds of years,' he replied with confusion.

'While you're living in rainbow land somewhere planning to take us out from your jealousy, you obviously haven't worked out what the bigger issue is,' Adam was now finally getting somewhere.

'Enlighten me sir,' William said without a care in the wold, he was so naïve.

I was starting to feel repulsed by his scent, which grew worse the longer he was in my restraint.

'Hunters are back and they are gaining in on us closer, and before you ask, it's Zak, so there is no way we can bury our heads in the sand and hide this time,' Adam had a point, but I was not sure what he was trying to achieve by having a conversation with a new breed, my first impression of William did not give much hope for the rest.

'Get this kitten off me and maybe I may just hear you out,' William replied, wiggling his arms.

'Chloe stand down, that's an order,' Adam firmly ordered.

'I'm no kitten,' I said, as I removed my hard grip.

William took a deep breath and brushed himself off. He had bright red marks on his wrists; he moved his head side to side and stared at Adam. 'So what you're saying is, we work together to get Zak and his men, and then we will have our fight another day,' William said, almost laughing, being sarcastic, but no one else found it funny. All eyes were on William; he looked to the ground and rubbed his pale chin.

'You do realise I'm only the messenger. What you don't realise is, if I go back and tell them what you told me today and they don't like it or believe me, they will remove my position or even cut me off from the pack,' he laughed again. 'You must think I'm very silly,' William finished.

'What if we go with you and explain the situation? Perhaps me and Brad could go, Adam?' Rob asked, looking at Adam.

'What do you think William?' Adam asked.

'Suicide if you ask me, if I take you with me they won't listen to you. Perhaps you're alpha Adam, but they will only listen to the true bloodline,' William said, speaking for the first time without a smirk or hint of laughter. Adam did not look amused with William saying an alpha shouldn't go. 'So I guess we won't be going, seeing as it would be impossible to find a true bloodline in time, what a shame,' William said with sarcasm.

'You're wrong, we will be going,' I said. Everyone turned towards me.

'Ha ha, you mean to say you have the true bloodline running through your veins? Impossible, you're like a cat that cannot be trained,' he replied.

I got up close to William's face and stared him in the eye, 'Me and my cousin Ben are few of the remaining, and I'm not a kitten.' I walked back two paces.

'So it's done William. Chloe, and Ben you will go find the others and negotiate and try to reason with them. William, will you stay with us while we take it in turns to hunt?' Adam asked nicely.

'I don't see that I have much choice, either I stay willingly or she's going to make me,' he replied and I grinned in amazement that he finally got it.

William stayed in the cave with Tim while I tried to hunt. This time I was completely on my own, the freshly rested snow made it easier to hunt down any animals close by. We could not hunt well as our human selves, it was impossible to keep up with, or sneak towards, our prey. I closed my eyes and tried to take myself to my thoughts, but it was taking too long. I tried harder, thinking right back to my old memories, thinking about Mum and even

Charlie. Nothing. I just couldn't feel my strange emotion; I hadn't had to force it since the day Ben started training me but today I couldn't get to it. The only thing I felt was a gaping hole in my chest, breathing without feeling. I wanted to feel sad, I wanted to feel pain for the part of me that was missing.

It'd been an hour trying to phase, trying to use all my thoughts to trigger me off, but still nothing. Walking back, feeling the one thing that was left, I felt only anger; I thought about how I was now incomplete. *If I can't phase, I can't fight ... or can I?* I had got super strength. I was quick. Really quick. It felt so natural how I'd picked William up with ease, only using one hand, *how much more am I capable of?* I asked myself. I realized my human skin wouldn't protect me from the new breeds if they decided to attack. *Yes, I heal quickly,* I thought, *but they could tear my foot of with the right grip for their jaw.* I needed new clothes, but I would have to tell Tim and he would tell the others. *This could mean Adam will stop me from going, I have to go.*

After much thought I entered the cave to find Tim standing and William crouched on the ground. 'Look what the cat dragged in,' William said with a huge smile. I narrowed my eyes and then turned to Tim.

'Can I have a word?' I asked Tim.

'Course,' he replied.

We walked around the corner not completely out of sight from William, but hopefully far enough that he could not hear.

'Something has happened; I don't have much time to explain. Can you keep a secret for me?' I asked.

'Yeah course, anything for you Chloe,' he said looking so kind, like he always did.

'The ancestor did decide to take from me, my blood wasn't all they wanted. They took the animal within me, I can't phase or feel. But in return I have been given strength, speed, and fast healing,' I paused.

'Wow. Ok, so what now?' he asked with compassion.

'I need to protect myself, we both know our human skin can easily be pierced, yes I can heal quickly but I don't know how quickly. Can you do me a big favor?' I asked him again. He nodded.

'I need protective clothing, something I can move fast in. I need weapons, I'm thinking a blade or two. You're going to have to find me a holder to put them in.' I pulled out a credit card and handed it to him, he didn't respond at first.

'Weapons, Chloe! We don't use weapons we use our hands, it totally against what we stand for!' Tim sounded cross.

'I don't have a choice! You must! You are our provider and I'm asking you as a favor for me, there is a fighting and hunting shop near the edge of town. You will find weapons and accessories there, or try a motor bike store for light protective clothing. Leather would be the best option, and some boots that go past the ankles, I think that should do it.'

'Is that everything?' he asked not looking so friendly now but disappointed.

'Thank you,' I replied and Tim exited through the tunnel, leaving me with William.

'Someone has upset their ancestors. Tut, tut,' William began to talk.

'Enjoy the conversation did you?' I asked

'Well yes it was very interesting, so that's why you're a super kitty with attitude hmm?'

'You know nothing,' I snapped back

'No Chloe, you my dear know nothing, you don't even know who you are do you?'

A part of me just wanted to switch off and ignore William, the posh creep. *Of course I know who I am, who does he think he is to tell me otherwise!*

'I'm Chloe, British, part of the black legends. And yes, you did hear the correct word, legend,' I smirked.

'Yes but you also take orders from your so called alpha, but everyone knows true bloodlines are alpha and certainly don't take orders. There aren't so many of you so the bigger person wins the title. Adam really is a nobody,' he said playing with a silver ring on his finger.

I felt William's words were lies, I did not trust him and nor did I think anything he had said was him being honest. I looked at him, and then turned my head looking anywhere but at him.

'Oh dear, cat got your tongue,' he said so slyly.

'No but I'll cut out yours,' I said standing up. 'Why do you smell so bad anyway?' I asked him.

'You don't smell too good yourself,' he snapped back.

'Ok, why are you different to us?' I asked him.

'Really do I have to answer that question? Practically everyone knows and it's embarrassing,' he replied looking right away from my direction. I didn't answer, I wanted to know why. He said that they were more superior and as far as I could tell they weren't as scary as the others made out to be.

'Ok! I will tell you, but you cannot mock me. You see, many years ago back when your ancestors were protecting the villagers, before hunters came about, we hadn't been created yet by my ancestors. One fellow legend came up with the idea that we shouldn't have children with humans. He said that we should only breed with our own kind, 'cause, as you already know, there aren't many female legends, only ones that are part of the bloodline. Of course this made an alpha angry because he had fallen in love with a human villager, and he wanted a family. They said it would be too dangerous as they couldn't know the outcome, but he did it anyway. He promised her that she would have superior babies that would walk the earth like warriors,' William paused, his eyes filled with sorrow as he took a deep breath and continued.

'She believed him and eight months later, the legends discovered the pregnancy and wanted to kill her before it was too late. But the couple vanished and left the village into the wild. He brainwashed her to believe they were making a difference, but she didn't understand why they had to run,' William paused again.

'What happened next?' I asked

'She had a hard time at child birth as she was bringing her babies into the world, things didn't go to plan. They weren't like any other cubs; their skin was red and their fur was the purest grey-white they had ever seen. She had three new born and only two survived,' William shook his head and looked at me.

'What happened to the two that survived?' I asked, intrigued.

'I don't know what exactly happened but apparently the alpha ran off shouting, "It's a monster." The mother brought her babies up in secret; of course once her children were old enough one sought revenge. That's why there are so many of us, he got busy,' William finished.

'Ok, so really you're just like us? Just not in appearance,' I asked with interest.

'Hmm we will never be like you; we don't have sick ancestors that cast people away to exile. We had only had two and she gave them a chance,' William said in short temper.

I didn't know who I felt sorry for, if I could even feel sorrow, I crouched down in front of William.

'We are not them, you have no one left to avenge they died years ago,' I looked directly into his bright, blue eyes. He didn't say anything straight away, he put his head down and then looked into my eyes.

'We weren't made for anything else but revenge against your kind,' he responded

Made, ok made, made could have several different meanings. 'When you say made, you do you mean born for revenge?' I asked.

This information didn't make sense to me, maybe I didn't know as much as I should. He laughed and almost snorted and smiled, it was almost false.

'Chloe dear, I was not born this way. You honestly don't know anything do you? Oh this is becoming very awkward,' he said, making me look stupid!

I'd listened to Adam and Ben, but I hadn't really asked questions I just wanted to get to know myself first and then got chucked in the deep end regarding enemies. I shook my head looking down, how could he not be born one of us? There wasn't any other way! I frowned in disbelief.

'I was once a young boy brought up by a wealthy family in a big house down in paradise bay, north side of San Francisco. I was only fourteen when I was taken, at the time I was achieving top grades and awards on science projects. When he took me I thought, "Why me?" Was it ransom money he wanted? It was my potential he was after; I don't remember much because I block it out. All I remember is being scared and then pain, next day I didn't have a care in the world,' William finished his story.

Silence passed and Tim entered the room holding bags in his hand. Tim didn't look too impressed and passed the bags over. 'Tell Adam or I will,' Tim warned me.

Death Mountain

I was standing outside the cave taking in worthless breaths, wondering if Adam would consider letting me fight under the circumstances. I couldn't help but think about William and his past and the information he enlightened me with.

He didn't have to say much else, it was obvious that the new breeds could pick and choose who they wanted to join them, brainwashing their soul 'til there was nothing left but revenge. *How can they change them?* I wondered. Why hadn't Adam or Ben told me the truth about our enemies? And was it true that me and Ben should be leading the pack. Also how come some of us weren't a descendent to the bloodline, were we much different from them? I needed answers.

'Chloe what are you wearing?' Brad giggled, of course they would be wondering why I was dressed like this.

Tim managed to find exactly what I was looking for; being covered in black leather clothing head to toe would be quite a statement. My boots passed my ankles, with laces that crossed over one another, my jacket was fitted with a zip to the left side with sliver studs on the small shoulder pads. Trousers that were skin tight; he managed to find them with a sheep skin front and flexible fabric inside. I was not very educated in materials but these were very comfortable and, I was guessing, expensive. The card I gave Tim was registered to Aunt Jane's house. Which gave me great pleasure thinking about when they came looking for the repayments.

I ignored Brad and looked at Ben by his side; I needed to talk to Adam but not before I confided in Ben first. Walking over to him I looked at Brad and moved my head to the direction that Brad should be continuing walking to.

'Fine,' he snapped at me. 'Attitude,' he whispered as Brad headed to the cave.

I held Ben's arms, he looked confused and cross.

'Chloe what has happened to you? After the ritual we are all fine, but you, you're different. The way you were with William scares me; you could have seriously hurt him and you couldn't care less,' he said holding my arms and pushing them away.

'I want to explain myself to you before I ask Adam the truth, the ritual last night took something from me. You remember when I found you and you were teaching me how to phase and control?' I asked.

'Yes, of course, but what does this have to do with ritual?' he replied.

'They took my feelings, my emotions, everything that helps me to phase, they left me like this. I cannot phase, Ben, I don't know what to do, I'm even wearing this to protect myself,' I looked to the floor wanting to feel something, just something that was supposed to feel natural.

'I'm sorry, I didn't realise I just thought you were annoyed about passing out over the whole ritual. It makes sense now, can never understand you women sometimes,' Ben sounded very sorry for me.

'So what now? Do I tell Adam and he will push me to the side, stopping me from fighting?' I asked, but Ben just smiled.

He put his hands on my shoulders, realised the studs were pointy and took them back again.

'It's clear to me you are still capable of defending yourself after the performance earlier. I have rabbit to share as always,' he grinned.

'Thanks,' I laughed back, and we walked back together.

After we ate our meals, William talked about science and evolution and the pack listened to him. It was time for some rest, I decided not to tell Adam yet and hoped Tim would give me time. I knew Adam would answer the questions going through my mind, but we needed to get the new breeds sorted first, before they came looking for a fight. William should have been back by now; their alpha would think we had taken him hostage, which we kind of had. Everyone said their 'good night's and the cave went into complete darkness.

'Morning,' I heard, looking up to see William staring down at me.

I sat up resting my elbow on my knee looking at him, cross.

'Ah you're not a morning person I take it? Or a day or night person for that matter,' he joked.

Adam walked into the room with the others behind him. 'Chloe, Ben and William you all head out today, we don't have much time before they send out a search party,' he commanded.

'We don't even know where we are going, what we are going to say or how will we convince them,' I said with concern in my voice.

'I've prepped Ben, he knows the score. William, you lead the way and they will follow, but you lead them down and wrong path and I'll let them do what they need to put you back in place,' he looked at William with narrow eyes and a frown. William gasped then laughed at Adam. It was clear that we were all getting fed up with how William dealt with threats.

'Shall we?' William held out his hand to help me up.

I ignored his gesture and stood on my own, I nodded at Adam in agreement with the new task at hand. Rob grabbed my arm before I went, with no one looking, 'Trust no one,' he said, and let go of my arm. It was strange for Rob to talk to me, especially when it was a warning, as he had always been reserved with me.

We walked north up towards the bank by the main road which led to Jane's house. Ben looked back towards me in confusion.

'No, we do not use roads,' Ben shouted to William.

'If we don't cross over it, it will take us a lot longer to get there,' William said seriously to Ben.

'It's fine, no one will see us,' I said to Ben as we climbed up the banks and looked through the bushes, a few cars passed us up and down. It was very early so there were only the few people, who lived in the area, who would use the road.

Rushing across the road as quickly as we physically could we continued our journey, not knowing where we were going or how long it was going to take to get there. We started picking up the pace until we were running and jumping over fallen trees and through ferns and bushes, untouched terrain. We had been travelling for two hours straight without stopping.

'Wait!' I shouted to Ben and William, but they didn't hear me, I could hear the ground disturbed over to my left. I could see the ferns moving, and I could smell something delicious. It smelled familiar, I wasn't going to wait to find out what it was.

I slowly reached down to grab my blade from my support belt that was resting on my thigh. I took a deep breath and leapt into the fern, I didn't look to see who it was straight away, without much thought I was behind his back with my blade touching his neck.

He wasn't scared I could sense it, he wasn't surprised either. I was considering my next move. It all happened so fast I didn't give myself much time to think. 'Chloe,' he whispered, I moved the blade from his neck and tightened my arm round his neck.

'Who are you?' I demanded.

'It's me Charlie,' he continued to whisper. I dropped my blade in shock, *how could I not tell that was Charlie? I could sense him a mile off, I only saw him a couple of days ago and now it's like I don't even know him.* He turned and looked at me all concerned and kissed my forehead. *Could it be butterflies and warmth I can feel? Oh my, I can feel again!* I smiled. It was a miracle. I put

136

my arms around him and made the most of the moment I had with him. He pushed me back and the feeling was gone, the hole in my chest was back. For one moment I felt the old Chloe was alive, but then darkness.

'I had to find you to tell you, Zak has been busy planning his attack. There are around six hunters with him, the more time he has the more he can gather to join him. The only chance you have is to stop them now before Zak has an army. He is in Canada at the moment heading this way,' he pleaded.

'Canada is a long way away, we have time,' I replied calmly.

'But you haven't, each day he is getting more powerful. You don't have much of a chance now let alone if he gathers ten more men by then,' he spoke urgently.

I looked at Charlie, then took a deep breath and looked him straight in his beautiful eyes, 'We have a chance, not the best I know, but we are stronger than ever and more determined,' I replied.

'Chloe!' Ben shouted in the distance.

Charlie kissed me again and put his finger on my lips to be quiet and then stood and started to run in the opposite direction. I couldn't tell Charlie our plans, he would stop us and I couldn't have the only chance we got taken, I couldn't let us down.

'Here!' I shouted back, I walked out of the ferns and bushes.

'What do you think you are doing? We don't have time for hide and seek,' Ben moaned.

'I had to pee, jeez!' I lied, I walked towards him and William looked at me with a grin on his face and his arms crossed, I walked past him, giving him daggers.

We continued to run forward with a fast pace, so fast the trees beside us looked like a green blur. William held his hand up to stop us, he pointed up. Little did me and Ben know what was installed. Looking up through the trees there was a huge mountain so tall the summit was in the clouds.

'Hope you both like climbing,' William said. Ben looked at me with one eyebrow raised, he didn't look too impressed. 'Phasing is the best way up to climb and quicker,' William said much to my disadvantage.

'No,' I snapped, they both looked at me puzzled. 'We will do it as we are,' I said sternly, this time I had raised both eyebrows.

'Too worried about leaving your new clothes behind?' Williams said and giggled, just as I thought I could get along with William he proved me wrong. William knew I couldn't phase, he heard mine and Tim's conversation, *what is he playing at?*

'Yes, I'm worried about my clothes,' I replied through my teeth.

'Chloe I'm surprised at you,' Ben said jokingly.

'So be it, we will climb this death mountain with two feet,' William said as he walked toward the gigantic mountain, *why death mountain*? I wondered.

We got to a small narrow foot path. 'We shouldn't be using public paths,' Ben moaned, I looked at him and took my first steps up the mountain. I felt like an ant climbing up a huge ant hill. After the long run I felt energy draining from me, this would not be good if we needed it for a fight.

Time had passed and we had reached the end of the footpath where it was no longer safe to walk. I took a seat on a rock looking out to the amazing view, the lake was glistening in the sun, birds were flying high and the snow slowly disappearing on low ground.

'Get up,' Ben shouted at me and walked over to grab my arm.

'No, we need to rest before we meet them. How do we know this plan is going to work and we won't need to fight them?' I said, concerned.

'No offence taken,' William joked waving his hands. Ben sat next to me looking out to the glorious view.

'You're right, sorry I'm just worried and not thinking,' Ben replied.

We had been sat down for an hour regaining our strength. 'How far now William?' Ben asked.

William looked at him and stood up and hummed, moving his head to the side, making it look obvious that he was thinking. 'We are approximately five minutes away,' he said with a smirk.

'You what!?' Ben shouted, angry we were so close. William laughed.

'Why did we have to phase if it's just up a foot path?' I asked with anger.

William shrugged, 'More fun I guess.' I was ready to punch him when Ben jumped between us.

'Save it Chloe,' Ben said with calmness while looking at William in disgust.

William walked on up towards the big rocks and made his way across, free-climbing up. 'Don't look down,' he laughed and continued. I looked at Ben and followed William's lead trying to put my hands and feet exactly where he put his. Looking down wasn't the most scary part, it was following William that was. I still didn't trust him and his rock climbing ability. I put my left foot where William had his and my right arm on a rock above and started pushing myself up. Carrying my body weight wasn't a problem, I could only imagine how hard it was for humans, even the strongest of them all would struggle.

'Ben how you doing?' I called to him keeping my eyes above.

'Fine, let's just keep going,' Ben replied, he didn't sound too far below.

'Almost,' William called. I could see a ledge not too far away; from the ground you wouldn't know it was there just hidden. I could start to feel my body ache, with all of the physical activity today it wasn't a surprise. *No matter how strong you are your body will only take so much,* I tell myself, it was the only thing that reminded me, that something, somewhere inside of me was still a human being.

I could see William climbing onto the ledge and sitting down ready for me to catch up, he looked so at ease, being so high up. I wondered how long he had been there, taken from his family.

'Give me your hand, I'll pull you up,' William called. I looked at him trying to judge whether he was genuinely trying to give me a help up. I waited for a moment looking into his blue eyes, he narrowed his eyes and held his hand out further.

'Chloe just grab his hand I don't think I can hold much longer,' Ben shouted. Taking one final push up, I grabbed William's hand, he gripped on tight and pulled me up. I sat to the side of the ledge while we waited for Ben, William helped him up and Ben nodded at him in appreciation.

'William there's nothing up here, why?' I shouted in anger. All I could see was rocks and one big rock in the middle, it was a dead end.

'It's no dead end, petal,' he replied. Him calling me petal made my skin crawl, and he knew it. William put both hands on the middle rock pushing the rock inwards.

'Don't just watch Chloe let's give him a hand,' Ben commanded.

'Uh,' I sighed. With the three of us now using full strength against the gigantic rock it started moving enough to see light coming from the other side.

'One more push,' William shouted with all that he had. The rock was moving; I began to push harder with all my might. 'That's it, that's it,' William said as he moved away. I looked at Ben in hope that he could see just how irritated I was, he nodded.

'Follow me quickly, there would have been someone on their way to warn them by now and best we get there when they do.'

'Chloe I'm going to phase, you stay as you are,' Ben says.

'Obviously,' I replied sharply.

'Sorry I know it must be hard for you, I'll be right by your side, just make sure you stick to the plan. We want them to ally with us, so behave,' Ben said with a grin. I continued to follow William into the open, behind the rock wasn't what I thought it would be. I'd only ever expect a cave in the mountain, but it wasn't. It was damp and dark and snow was everywhere, huge rocks stood to either side of a path that looked made.

'Hang on why has he phased? Not part of the plan,' William shouted. His arms were crossed and his head was to the side again.

'Protection,' I said slyly, it gave me satisfaction to annoy him.

The rocks began to widen with more open space, William stopped and waited. He put his hands up to stop us from getting closer to him, for someone not feeling anything, I was sure I could feel the tension and William's nerves. I could feel the same sensation Williams scent gave me, only that bit more potent.

'It's me William,' he called, I looked ahead waiting. I saw these red eyes peeking from inside the rocks in front of William. He lowered his head and bent onto one knee, like he was in submission.

'You have not come alone I see,' I heard a deep voice echoing. It went silent, William lifted his head up.

'No master, they have come with a proposal,' William said softly. *Master?* I wondered, *how very formal*. It was almost pleasurable to see William not acting like the big shot.

'And you feel this proposal is worth risking your life? Hmm William?' the echo got louder. I looked to my left and Ben was right by my side, close; he looked at me and showed some teeth. I guessed Ben was feeling the tension too. *Who is the master?* I wondered.

'Yes,' William replied.

'Yes who?' the echo said.

Without a pause William corrected himself, 'Yes master.'

Looking into the darkness I could see the red eyes moving closer, a pale face appeared. His hair was blonde like William's and his eyes were a pinky-red colour, he had skin so pale you could see dark shadows under his eyes and cheek bones. He rubbed his chin. 'Who are you young lady?' he called.

'Chloe, and this is Ben, we are from Adam's pack, from south of here. And who might you be?' I asked without hesitation.

His eyebrow raised in disbelief. 'I am Tate, alpha of the new breeds I have created. Everyone before you belongs to me,' he raised his arm up, looking around, little had I noticed lots of monsters were surrounding us.

Looking just like us, but different, their eyes were various colours. Some of their fur was rough and some was smooth and shiny. Then the colour of their coat was between snow-white and grey. They looked bloodthirsty like they hadn't eaten in days. I looked back to Tate, without showing any fear.

'So what on earth brings you here? It must be something important to risk all three of your lives. Believe me when I tell you I would not hesitate to assassinate every single one you, you're making me want to puke with your sweet stench,' his nose screwed up in disgust.

'We have trouble and not just us, on ground. We are all in danger,' I said, hoping he was taking me seriously.

Tate crossed his arms and tapped his foot, and nodded his head. 'See that's where you are wrong you are on the ground we aren't, we were safe 'til William decided to bring you here,' Tate walked up closer to William. William still had not moved from the ground. He looked back to the floor. 'I thought you were a clever boy William, in all my years have I ever came across someone so stupid?' his voice was raised, and angry towards William.

'We kept William hostage and forced him to bring us over to you, he had no choice. It's the hunters,' I began as Tate cut me off raising his hand.

'Huh,' he sighed. 'Hunters you say? They haven't been round here for a while. Well only the odd one passing through, what do they want this time aye? You?' Tate asked.

I shook my head. 'All of us, every single one of our kind. It's been planned for weeks, maybe months, for their arrival to Alaska. I know what you're thinking Alaska a big place, right?' I stopped. Tate was still listening and the others hadn't moved. I continued, 'They know exactly where to find us and it won't be long 'til they find you, you see they don't want us to exist.'

He cut me off again raising his hand, 'Tell me something I don't already know, like why you are here disturbing us. Like you can just visit,' Tate said to me sharply.

144

He was losing patience I could feel it, only me blabbering was not going to help matters.

'Ok,' I raised my hand up. 'I'll get straight to the point. We need you to fight back with us, if we work together we can defeat Zak and his cult. Put aside our differences and we'll have our fight another day, we know you want us dead too but if you don't help us you're as good as dead like the rest of us!' I pleaded. Begging wasn't my style, nor would that change today, Tate would not get the satisfaction today nor ever.

'How do I know we will not be doing all the hard work and you're just coming here to get us to do your dirty doings? Hmm. Maybe you're weak and afraid, or maybe you're just trying to trap us on the surface. Zak doesn't just come for a visit, he's like an army with the taste for blood. It's victory, not just the hunt he wants, and you think I'll risk all my hard work just so you can kill all my men while you bathe in the glory if we succeed?' Tate said, and laughed and looked to his creatures. He started walking around William and paused. Tate struck him hard across his face. William continued to stay still and didn't even flinch, like he was used to the pain.

'It isn't like that! If you do not help us or yourself you're a coward, to you these men are just toys! They had a life once and you took it and now you won't give them a chance to defend their new selves because you still feel threatened by us? How pathetic that a man can still hold a grudge, hundreds of years on,' I argued. Ben nudged his head against my leg, if he could talk right now I was guessing I'd be told to notch it down a peg.

'Feisty one you are, hey?' he said as he walked closer to me rubbing his hands together, more of a creep than William was. 'Ok here is the deal, I let you keep William 'til I make up my mind. Either way we will come, for the three of you and the rest of your stupid weak pack, or to fight. I'm guessing you'll have to wait and find out princess,' Tate finished and waved his hand to his men to follow, he walked back into the darkness laughing.

I looked to Ben and his head was facing the ground in disbelief. Even though I felt pretty much nothing, I could feel the feeling of dread for my pack and others. We could have made things a hundred times worse! *What if I have?* I wondered.

William stood up brushed himself off and turned to us shaking his head. 'Let's go,' he said, cross, and pushed his way between us.

We followed back down the same passage we came in, only this time less hopeful. Ben stopped near his pile of clothes and we walked away to give him privacy; even though no one really cared anymore I still felt if there was time for privacy it was nice to have for a change.

William went over first to the ledge, then myself, then Ben. I didn't notice anyone following us too close to the opening, *I guess they aren't so efficient after all.*

'Nice one Chloe, now we might as well all jump off this mountain,' William snapped looking down.

Ben put his hand on my spiky shoulders again, and quickly removed them. 'It's not your fault Chloe, we all knew it's wasn't going to be easy to persuade them to help, you really need a new jacket,' Ben joked.

'It is new,' I smiled. William did not look impressed with mine and Ben's banter. *How do we get down?* I wondered looking over the edge.

'We go down same way we came up,' William announced much to mine and Ben's disapproval.

Hollow Heart

We got down to the bottom of the mountain, our journey back was quiet. William hardly said a word just sulking about his misfortune. Walking back through the forest was so peaceful, and pleasant. I couldn't imagine my life with my own room and bed and a hot shower or a soak in the bath, even just enjoying the fresh towels. Being indoors just felt like a cage. *It's funny I never thought I'd understand how a dog feels,* I chuckled to myself.

'What's so funny?' Ben asked.

'Do you ever wonder what it would be like being back in a house again?' I asked him.

'Trapped animal springs to mind!' William answered my question. I laughed without caring that it was William who answered.

'Exactly what I was laughing at,' I pointed to William. Ben still hadn't answered my question, I paused, waiting, but he didn't look like he wanted to participate.

'Being back in a house isn't a choice anymore, whether I fantasised about it or not Chloe, I'm just glad to have you and my brothers. A house wouldn't be a home without you all,' Ben finally replied.

'You're lucky!' William said with jealousy. 'I had a family and a home and now I have nothing I haven't for years. You're right about Tate. We are just his toy men.'

I suddenly realised maybe William had just been bitter with jealousy.

'If Tate wasn't around we wouldn't stay. A lot of us thought about going alone but he said the legends would kill us, stupid right?' William asked.

'Not stupid, just not well educated about us. We aren't evil and dwelling on the past. All we want is peace and to enjoy our animal instincts,' Ben answered.

We were getting closer to the road, the walk felt longer from the mountain. 'Do we make a run for it?' I asked Ben.

He walked ahead of me, 'There's something I need to do and have needed to do for a long time,' he replied and started walking along the road.

'You're crazy,' William shouted to Ben.

'Go back to the others both of you!' Ben commanded.

'I'm not going anywhere,' I replied. I knew exactly where he was heading and couldn't have forgiven myself if anything were to happen.

'Suit yourself,' William said as he darted across the road and dived into the bushes.

'Are you sure Ben? She's not the same mother you ran from,' I said hesitantly.

He continued walking on with powerful strides. 'I don't care anymore; I want to see her face one last time. Remember the face that disowned us in the fight,' he answered.

I couldn't help but wonder exactly what was he thinking of, *has he lost the plot? What if she is not alone?* 'Ben, wait!' I shouted. He stopped and turned back to face me, looking annoyed. 'What if she's not alone? Zak could already be here,' I asked hoping he would consider the possibilities.

'You're either with me or not, I'm doing this.'

We approached Aunt Jane's house, it looked abandoned, with an overgrown garden. She was a house-proud woman; I couldn't imagine she would have just sat back and watched her home fall from perfection. We walked up the path to the front door, it was slightly open. I looked at Ben's face to work out what he was feeling or thinking, he just looked more determined to find her. He pushed the door open and walked in. It was dark and a complete mess. Jane's art work everywhere, a lamp knocked over.

We continued to check the house; the kitchen had dirty plates smashed on the floor with mould on the unclean pieces. The tap was dripping and fridge wide open, it looked like a struggle happened in the kitchen and the hall way. The phone was off the hook dangled in the air. I walked towards the lounge to find Ben; he stood completely still staring to the corner. 'Ben,' I called. No answer.

I walked closer to him. 'Ben,' I whispered, he still ignored me. Creeping up closer behind him to see what he was looking at, I peered over his shoulder. I gasped at the horrific view, a beaten old lady, her face black and blue with one eye swollen shut. She was staring at Ben with her good eye, her arm touching her lower rib and one leg resting on a wooden leg rest. You could see her bruises on her ankles. I wanted to feel ashamed of myself for not feeling any remorse for her.

'Hello son,' she said with some difficulty. Ben still froze without any signs of response.

'What happened?' I asked.

She turned her head slowly to my direction. 'And wouldn't you like to know, little miss I'm-so-perfect!' she replied with hatred. I was far from perfect but I hadn't got a clue why she felt I was.

'What happened to you?' I asked again, more firmly.

She looked back at Ben. 'You going to let her talk to me like that son?' she said sarcastically.

Ben bit his lips and rubbed his neck. He whispered, 'It's no less than you deserve,' in spite.

'Speak up,' she snapped, leaning forward in her chair.

'It's no less than you deserve you witch!' he shouted with his arms shaking in rage, his mouth pressed together tightly.

She sat back in her chair, looking at me. She'd become more bitter and twisted; I didn't want to give her the time of day.

'Let's go Ben clearly she wishes to be alone,' I grabbed Ben's arms slowly and walked him towards the door.

Ben was still not very responsive; the room was quiet and the only sound was the floorboards' creaking as we slowly walked away.

'That's it Chloe, take him away, don't want him finding out about your special boyfriend hmm? What is that saying again?' Jane shouted at me in spite again.

I stopped and turned in shock, *how does she know about Charlie? What if Ben finds out?* I ignored her and grabbed Ben's arm again to walk him out.

'"Sleeping with the enemy", ah that's the saying. What's it like Chloe lying to your family, betraying them, keeping secrets?' she laughed.

'Maybe I should ask you what it's like!' I said quickly and walked Ben out the door.

He dropped down and sat on the porch, I sat next to him and looked at his face. He turned his face and I didn't think I had ever seen him look so angry with me.

'Is it true?' he asked. I couldn't answer. I could not lie to his face nor could I tell the truth. 'Who is it? You will answer me now Chloe! If you don't I will make Adam force it out of you,' he commanded.

'You wouldn't understand, and you certainly wouldn't want to listen to what I have to say because you would not want anything to do with me,' I pleaded. There was an awkward silence while waiting for his reply. I hated Jane even more than I ever thought I could. She knew exactly what effect this would have on the pack, *it's perfect! Exile the strong one so the pack is more vulnerable. Clever.* I thought.

'His name is Charlie, I met him before I knew who I was. It was when I started getting the changes that he showed up. I know you won't want to know this, but he is so desirable. He smells wonderful and looks perfect, I was drawn by my instincts. At the time I didn't know who he was or who I was, had not a clue,' I realised I was not in the wrong for falling for Charlie, how was I to know back then he was a hunter?

'When did you stop seeing him, when you realised?' Ben asked forcefully.

I bowed my head in shame, it would break his heart that I'd betrayed them all. 'No, it was too late,' I replied pretending emotion to cover my lack of feelings. He shook his head in disbelief. He put his head in his hands and at that moment I saw weakness, the kind of weakness that only someone you really cared about could make you feel. 'He's been helping me, telling me Zak's moves and watching over us,' I said soothingly.

Ben looked up into the distance and crossed his arms over his knees, 'We don't need help from his kind. Jesus Chloe how careless are you? He could turn on you any time, I can't lose you, you're all the family I have left. Promise me you won't see him again? And cut loose of any strings or feelings you have,' Ben said, without anger or shouting.

I couldn't feel emotions anyway for now, but I wanted to feel the love I had for Charlie again. Love was a strong word; I might never get the chance to tell Charlie how I felt. I would not imagine my life without him, but I could never betray my family. I pictured in my mind being pulled apart, with Ben and Charlie either side. *But why is Ben so calm, maybe he knows. A connection like a magnet that forces you together, perhaps he understands?* I wondered.

'You know it's not as easy to let go of people you care about, I will try, I can promise this to you Ben. But right now we need to focus on our enemies not my not very existent love life,' I pleaded to Ben. *He must understand Charlie isn't the enemy;* But I'd been kidding myself to believe a male legend could become acquaintances with a hunter. It was hard enough when we got William, let alone a hunter joining us.

'Ok, you're right, but if I see him anywhere near you, you cannot judge me for my actions, you got that?' Ben reasoned. I smiled in relief and stood up and held out my hand for Ben. He looked up and smiled back and grabbed my hand and stood up. He let go and we began to walk down the path, I looked left and right at the road and ran and jumped into the bushes and rolled and jumped up to my feet. Ben was still right by my side. We took a slow walk and made the most of the peace and quiet, before we would have to see motor-mouth William.

The sun was shining and the snow still slowly melting, it had lost its fluffiness and become more slushy, with a hint of green poking through from the ground beneath.

'Chloe you know what?' he asked. *Hmm trick question?* I wondered to myself.

'What?' I replied.

'I think I like this new you,' he smiled. I nudged his shoulder and laughed, he laughed with me.

'Wanna race me?' I winked.

'It's on, first one to the edge of the lake wins?' he replied.

'Ok in one, two, three!' And within a flash we were off. Everything around me was just a blur when I ran with all I had; I could see Ben in the corner of my eye just a few small paces in front.

I tried harder and harder catching up, I was now just slightly ahead. We passed the training ground and were getting closer, we were now shoulder to shoulder. *Just one more push!* My legs could not go any faster. Ben slowed down a fraction, *got you,* I thought. I saw the lake in sight. *Problem is how am I supposed to go really fast to get to the edge of the lake without falling in? Perhaps that's why Ben is slowing down,* I tried slowing myself down in time. I skidded closer to the edge and stopped just in time, I took a deep breath in relief. I looked over and Ben was by the edge to. I was so concerned about falling in I forgot about the race.

I got my breath back and turned to Ben. 'Who won?' I asked, he laughed loud, uncontrollably, I hadn't seen Ben like this for many years.

'Oops,' he said, laughing again.

'What do you mean, "Oops"? Who won? Did you?' I asked again.

He slowed down and got his laughter back under control. 'I don't know,' he shrugged his shoulders.

I smiled and also laughed, we must have looked so stupid if anyone had seen us. 'Come, let's get back,' I said, although I didn't really want to rush back. We had been stuck in the cave for so long and had had no adventure 'til today, but it was starting to get dark and I was hungry. We started making our way back.

We had just entered the cave; the oil lamps were on and there was a fire roasting a rabbit on a spit. The pack were all sat on the ground talking, William was sitting aside from the others.

'You're back,' Tim noticed and smiled at me and Ben.

I looked towards William and he nodded with a grin. I walked towards Adam and took a seat down next to him.

'William has not really told us much, only that you stopped at the road, what happened with the new breeds?' he asked. William let out a sigh, and everyone looked at him. He didn't pay attention, he just looked to the ground.

'Their leader Tate didn't want to listen at first, he said that he will either be coming to fight with us or against us. So we didn't have much luck getting through to him, he is stubborn and not pleasant,' I told Adam.

Adam rubbed his chin and looked to me. 'Still a chance we might have some help hey?' he sounded positive.

'I wouldn't count on it,' William muttered under his breath. I still looked at William and found it hard to believe he wasn't born this way. *What's the difference between a true bloodline anyway, what makes me and Ben different from the others?* I wondered. I looked to Adam and moved closer, the others were busy talking and preparing food.

'Can I ask you something?' I asked Adam.

'Course,' he replied.

I took a deep breath, 'What is the meaning of true bloodline and not being true?' I asked.

Adam let out a deep breath like he knew one day we would wonder and ask. 'True bloodline is when you have come from a family of generations of legends from the beginning of when we were created. Not being true means someone along the line wasn't a true bloodline someone was transformed,' he looked into my eyes for a reaction. I looked blankly back; I found it hard to believe that the other members in the pack were different to Ben and me.

'So we can change ordinary people, just like how all the new breeds are created?' I asked, intrigued.

Adam didn't look comfortable talking about this subject, he seemed fidgety. 'Yes we can, but it's not an honourable thing to do. The pain and hurt, mentally and physically, is not the humane thing to put any living creature through. Not everyone can survive the transformation, many lives have been lost creating the new breed,' Adam looked down in disbelief.

'Did Tate kill many to get his new army?' I asked concerned.

He took in a large breath. 'He'd been hunting candidates for years, at first he would just take anyone from the street. People would die and he felt he was wasting time, so he made a note of the kind of people who wouldn't survive. He made progress with less loss; he noticed the people who died were ones that were weak and not very intelligent. See, being intelligent is important, the new breeds have to adapt to the changes fast in order to handle the process. Being strong and not so intelligent worked too, because the body is healthier and can manage pain easier. The heart can't handle the transformation without it.'

I pictured in my mind Tate standing over bodies shaking his head in disappointment and not caring of the lives he took. Blood on his hands and his creations locked up like animals. I began to wonder why they treated him like a master and would not want to kill him. How could you obey the man who stole your life and the people you care about?

'Did he ever transform females, because I never noticed any in the mountain?' I asked, more curious.

Adam seemed to feel more at ease as the conversation continued. 'No, he didn't want a distraction or for his creations to mate and have families, it would ruin the operation. Tate never had a true family and he despises the very thought of them. He could never love another with such hate in his heart,' Adam replied.

'So you know Tate well? Do you think his pride will stop him from helping us and himself?' I asked him.

The room went quiet like the whole pack is listening; Adam looked around to the others. 'Yes I know him well enough, I know he will stop at nothing to defeat us,' he responded.

William sat quietly still looking to the ground. It was as if he had had enough trying to defend or trying to irritate us.

'Why us?' Rob asked with mystery in his eyes, Rob was clever and I knew he asked with the intention of get to the point.

'Not us, me,' Adam replied bluntly. At this point everyone turned to face Adam and looked in shock, like this was new information to each of them. I'd thought I was the only one missing something.

'All this time you said they are after all of us, how could you lie and make us feel this is our fight?' Ben said with anger in his voice.

I could sense the rage in one another except William. I myself was shaking in anger, all I felt was anger inside, I didn't feel remorse for Adam at this moment in time.

'I am the alpha and you are my pack, if it's my fight it's all of your fight. You best remember who your loyalty lies with,' Adam defended himself sternly. 'Even if they did kill me they would make sure every single one of you was dead too. If I say it's my fight only that would be a lie too,' he finished. I could see it in his eyes: he was telling the truth.

'How did you and Tate become enemies?' I asked.

William stood up and walked out of the room, without explanation.

'I haven't always lived here, I'm from a town in the state of Washington. For your safety I do not want to go into specific detail, but I was the deputy sheriff. We worked hard to protect the town, day and night. There weren't serious crimes committed but we had enough to keep us busy, me and the sheriff. Sheriff Pete his name was. We were close, of course he didn't know my true self, anyway; people started going missing.'

The room was quiet listening to the story; the fire was burning bright. Adam briefly stopped and started again. 'We noticed a pattern forming, young men who went missing after they finished their jobs, no bodies found so we couldn't announce their death, but had to keep looking for evidence and clues. Pete started feeling the strain once the families were getting impatient. I started to wonder to myself if it could be supernatural, related, of course I couldn't tell Pete this. So after my shift I wouldn't go back to my apartment, I'd be out searching, using my instincts,' Adam's tale took a break again.

'I'd go on foot, catching scent from the last place they were seen. But it had been days, maybe weeks since they had been missing so the trails were hard to track. I'd continue to try as much as I could in my free time. One night I had a call from Pete telling me to be quick and get down to the local night club. One of the young boys on their team didn't show up to his shift, they only spoke to him that afternoon. I had a feeling he wasn't taken that long ago, so I jumped in my motor as quickly as I could. When I got there and stepped out I could smell it, the scent was unpleasant to the nostrils. Then I knew it was one of them, the story I was told growing up was true,' he finished.

He stared blankly as if he was too deep in his own memory.

'Adam,' I called softly, he blinked like he was back in the room.

'Sorry,' he said shaking his head. The others were still looking intense. I gave Adam a nod to continue.

'Sorry I lost my train of thought, I then followed the scent without realising Pete was following me. I got to an old abandoned animal shelter, I saw a glow of a candle in the gap of a blocked-out window. I crept around the building with a gun in my hand. Pete turned up behind me, I looked at him in surprise and he signalled me to be quiet.

'We arrived at a door and counted to three and kicked the door in. What we saw behind the door was horrifying, blood spilled on the floor and red hand prints splattered on the wall. Bodies piled up in the corner and people in cages. I remember the smell; it was awful and hard not to be sick. I had no idea he was behind us. Those eyes staring and the look of evil on his face, his mouth covered in blood. Before I could tell Pete to run it was too late he had bit him hard. He screamed so loud,' Adam nodded his head.

'Did he die?' I asked with wonder.

'No Chloe, he survived, but he suffered first. I had no choice but to kill every single one of his creations even though I knew they had families looking for them, Tate put up a fight at first but then made a run for it. I looked at Pete and didn't know if I should spare his life and see how it turned out or kill him and end his suffering,' he said with sadness in his voice.

'I killed him, so you see Tate wanted revenge for killing his creations and stopping him from taking more lives in my town, I didn't have a choice and I felt sadness for all the loss the town suffered so I made a run for it. On the news they said two local sheriffs were killed in a serial killer case,' he finished.

'So that's how you ended up here hidden away?' I realised Adam did the right thing protecting his town; it must have been such a burden having to kill the innocent. I could only imagine how what he saw that night stuck with him all this time. 'I'll fight for you,' I said standing up, I looked around to the others. They all started to stand with me.

'Me too,' Brad and Tim said.

'Count me in,' Ben added.

I looked at Rob and he seemed distant. 'I will fight but I am fighting for everyone, this still does not make up the fact you lied to us Adam but I will stand by you,' Rob said with honour.

'Thank you, yes I lied but I didn't want you to judge me. But now I see that I should know better and to trust you all more than I already do. We had better get some rest, tomorrow we hunt and track and check the perimeter. It won't be long 'til we have a fight on our hands, I want eyes everywhere 'til they arrive,' Adam finished and slumped down for a rest. We all sat back down to eat and closed our eyes and enjoyed the last peaceful night we would all have together.

Honesty

My eyes struggled to open, feeling heavy. The room was quiet as if no one was around me, all alone, so peaceful. I pictured Charlie in my mind, his beautiful face. A face I missed seeing and spending time with, *how can life be so cruel keeping us apart?* A magnetic force was being ripped apart from me; leaving a hollow feeling in my heart. Filled with such anger and pain, it was sometimes hard to remember to breathe when I felt so lost in my own world.

I lay there with no purpose to get up other than to fight, fighting with strength was great but fighting with love in our hearts was powerful. Without it I was just good, *but is it great enough to see us through?* I wondered. *I am a human with very little soul left I feel nothing in my heart and my strange emotions are gone, what does that make me?* Thinking of the negatives to help see the positives was hard; the only positive I could think of was a clear conscience on the battle field.

'Chloe get up! It's time to go,' Tim shouted, my eyes opened wide and I bounced up looking around.

I saw Tim looking over me in disappointment; he shook his head and walked on. It was clear he still didn't forgive me for not being honest with Adam and the others; little did he know Ben knew everything. *We don't have time for pathetic arguments about such a subject; it's because of Adam wanting to do the ritual that I'm like this in the first place,* I thought, mutinously.

I grabbed my jacket and walked towards the exit of the cave. As I walked towards the light I noticed the snow was nearly gone; just a few patches of white left, the lake still wasn't quite back to its usual temperature. I saw the pack talking in a group and William just sat on the ground in the distance, keeping out the way. I walked over to him.

'What you doing all the way over here? Shouldn't you be listening to Adam?' I asked William, he looked up still with the same expression as last night in the cave.

'He isn't my alpha, I don't take orders from him or any of you,' he said clearly, with aggression in his voice.

'Why do you still feel loyal to him?' I asked.

He put his head to the side looking at me blankly. 'He created me, I owe him my loyalty,' he replied like it was common knowledge.

'I don't understand, it makes no sense, why do you feel loyal to a man who ruined your life?' I was starting to get lost, I hadn't been so confused about loyalty ever. The others were still talking in a group, so I sat down next to him.

I asked him one more time 'Why?'

He still sat blankly. And then he turned to look at me, 'We don't choose this, you know that. We don't all know why we are loyal to Tate but he has some kind of hold on us. Don't trust me Chloe, we cannot be trusted, we are complicated. It's like he is in our heads giving orders without him being present. I'm better off on his side or dead because either way we won't get rid of him.' William talked with such loss and pain.

I looked over to the group, wondering what would happen to the pack once the battle was over. Would I still have them? Would I be alone like how William felt with us? I wanted to feel the worried like the others, I wanted to be normal, I wanted my feelings to be real and not to have to pretend to care or feel remorse.

'You say you can't be trusted but I can't help but want to trust you William. This may be the only time I can tell you this,' I paused as he looked at me with confusion, his forehead frowning. I couldn't help but find it amusing, the effect I had on him. 'I kind of hated your guts when I met you; I had the urge to kill you then. I would have if Adam hadn't shown up. Thing is that isn't me, I used to be soft and gentle and kind-hearted. I'm stuck between which Chloe I should be right now. The soft Chloe they need me to be, or the one who wants to kill everyone, which is the Chloe for the battlefield?'

William stopped frowning and put on the smirk that drove me crazy, the expression that nearly had him killed. 'Seeing as we are being open, I actually liked you from day one. I like the Chloe who wants to kill me not the one who you pretend to be to the others. You're fierce and strong and mainly brave, you'll make a good warrior in the fight. Tate is wary of you. Forget what they want you to be, be what they need you to be.'

Wow, that isn't the reply I would expect when you tell someone you wanted to kill them. He was right though, my strange emotion being gone was a gift from the ancestors. And I was going to use it.

We'd been walking around the lake and the surrounding areas all day, me and William stuck together. We crossed the others' paths a few times, much to Tim's disappointment. I didn't think he trusted William, which he had every right not to. But at least with William I didn't have to pretend.

I didn't like how me and Tim weren't so close anymore, it was like he knew I'd changed and had given up on me. We continued on further out from the lake, time felt like it stood still, noise around me stopped. One deep breath I inhaled, took the air right from my lungs.

'Charlie,' I whispered. I smelled him close, his intoxicating scent so enduring. It teased me. I started running and followed the scent, and right in front of my eyes his shadow was in the darkness of the forest. I stopped and smiled,

I felt an arm tugging on my shoulder. 'No Chloe, they'll see you,' William shouted pleading.

I shrugged his presence off, I moved towards Charlie as fast as a heartbeat. I saw his face and he was smiling back, he opened his arms ready to catch my embrace. I jumped in his arms, and held tight, he spun me around with the wind flowing through my long hair. He stopped spinning. I looked into his eyes and kissed him, I couldn't even think at the time, I just wanted him so badly.

I felt a slight flutter in my stomach, I paused. 'It can't be,' I said in surprise.

'What is it? Are you ok?' Charlie asked concerned.

I couldn't believe it, it had been a while without it but I knew for sure what I was feeling. *My strange emotion came back,* I thought to myself, *it can't be!* 'Oh no,' I said in horror.

'You're scaring me now,' Charlie spoke. *If I have my strange emotion come back, I'll be useless to my brothers.* William spoke sense earlier, in order to fight well I needed to be the tough Chloe. Which meant no Charlie, I had missed him so much, the last time I saw him was a blip. I stroked the hair hanging over his forehead back, and kissed him intensely for one last time.

'This is goodbye Charlie; I can't see you anymore. It's best you stay away 'til the fight is over,' I said with a tear rolling down my face.

He stroked it away from my cheek. 'It's ok, I will wait for you. I always will be in the shadow watching over you. Now go.' He smiled.

I turned around and started walking back to William, with every step I took I felt numb. I started shaking with anger in all of my body, just how I felt when I first lost my emotion.

'You can't be with him Chloe,' William said as I walked past.

'Let's go, you're right and leave it at that,' I snapped.

The rage in my head was beginning to become uncontrollable. I began running with everything I had, 'I want to hunt,' I told William. 'I need to hurt something; I need to get this rage out before heading back to the lake.'

It was usually better hunting with four legs, closer to the ground was better for tracking. At least I had my nose to follow. I went deeper into the forest; the ground didn't look too disturbed. William had phased. Looking closer, in more detail, I looked at him and thought to myself, *if someone had told me there were mystical or paranormal creatures living in the forest I'd have thought they were crazy*. His head came up to my waist; I could imagine a child could put a saddle on him and go for a ride. If they weren't scared of him of course. The wind blew and I could pick up a scent. William looked up at me, he must have caught it too, I could see William wanted to run before me.

'Ha it's on,' I shouted as I ran towards the scent, running was freedom, and right now I could hold on to the freedom and carry on running with it.

I saw a deer in sight, William wasn't far behind me. I knew he was catching up fast, but he wasn't taking my kill today. I leapt into the air and pulled out my knife from my sheath on my thigh. I pierced my knife straight into its neck; I saw life leave the deer's dark eyes. I pulled my knife back out and wiped it clean on my leg, I picked up the heavy lifeless deer and chucked it over my shoulder.

'Dinner is on me tonight,' I shouted to William. I turned my back for William to get clothed, he phased behind a bush and I was this pale arm go through the bush to pick up his clothes without me seeing him. I laughed hysterically, I found it hilarious. I'd seen every inch of my fellow pack, a sight that couldn't be unseen. I was sure his pale little bum wasn't going to stun me.

'Come on William, I'm hungry!' I shouted. He jumped up clothed, looking around, and he looked at me and grinned. We continued walking back and caught up with Tim and Brad. They hadn't seen us yet, or they just didn't want join us.

'Oi Tim,' I shouted to him, he turned and looked in disgust again. *He must still be upset I haven't told everyone yet. It's not his decision to make,* I thought frowning.

'What's his problem?' William said.

'Me not telling Adam what happen at the ritual,' I replied. I thought he would agree it was the right thing to do.

'You should tell them; you need to lead it's what you're born to do,' he said.

'Hang on one second, I don't want to lead. And why should I tell all of the others? You know and Ben knows and Tim knows. You all pretty much know,' I said in defence.

'Yeah but the alpha doesn't and he needs you, not the Chloe he knows the Chloe he needs to know, remember?' he tried to convey.

'Since when have you been smart?' I asked. *Damn,* I thought, *I prefer when we didn't talk, it's like he is always right! And it frustrates me.*

'Come on, I'm smart and handsome I can't see why it's hard to believe to have both,' he winked. I smiled and laughed. *He is smart and stupid, this one.*

We got to the lake and the others were waiting for us.

'Look what's for dinner,' Brad pointed to us.

'Woah not me,' William joked.

'Nice one Chloe,' Brad called over.

'I hope your hungry fellas,' I said, cocky. I was proud of my catch. We all walked to the cave with the sunset in sight, it was beautiful. The colours were so warm and the air so crisp. We picked up some firewood from outside the entrance before we headed in.

The fire was roaring while Rob was preparing the deer for us. The room was silent with everyone sat down. *I'm guessing it's now or never to be truthful*, I stood up. All eyes looked towards me. 'There's no easy way to say it so I'm just going to come out with it,' I spoke with confidence, Rob, Brad and Adam look concerned.

'The ritual took my emotions, my emotions that help me phase. I haven't phased since the ritual and haven't felt anything since. I'm stronger for it, there is nothing standing in my way anymore. You might think I'm useless or not fit to fight without phasing, but I'm more powerful and faster. At least I could communicate, and you can all phase readily,' I tried to convince myself and others.

'Out of the question, you cannot kill them without phasing,' Adam said, stern. I stood in silence waiting for Ben to back me up; I looked directly at him and gave him a nod of encouragement. Ben shook his head and couldn't give me eye contact, *coward*, I thought.

'She can, Chloe nearly killed me and she stood up to Tate. You can't see it can you, Mr big alpha! She's more of a fighter than you and all of you put together. Without her strength and courage and sacrifice you'd all be pretty screwed right now,' William spoke up on my behalf. I looked to William in surprise and looked back at the others. Brad and Rob's jaws were open in surprise and Ben looked at Adam for a reaction.

'So you have a voice for Chloe, I must say I am surprised due to how you both met. If our enemy can vouch for you, Chloe, and thinks you are to be feared then I don't have a choice but to let you. Remember this; your actions are on your shoulders if you should fail or be injured,' Adam spoke with honour.

The evening flew by with laughter and joy. William sat beside me joking and comparing strength, arm wrestling with each other. Others joked how we were new best friends, today me and William actually had created a bond. *It's funny how one minute you want to wring someone's neck and then you want to play around together.* Friendship formed when I least expected it, with the person I never thought possible.

'Thanks William, for earlier, I needed someone to back me up, I thought it would be Ben. Just shows how loyal to his alpha he is,' I said with gratitude.

'It's fine, end of the day I'm counting on you to keep me alive. Ok I know that sounds silly, but if Tate decides to fight against us at least I'll have one person on my side,' he said as we smiled together.

'Chloe,' Tim shouted from across the room. 'Come here?' he asked

I got up and walked over to him; he was standing next to the entrance to the waterfall. He was smiling from ear to ear looking pleased, Tim seemed happy again. 'Thank you Chloe so much, you have taken such a weight off my shoulders. I've been so worried about your secret. I'm glad you told Adam, he needs you more than he knows himself.' Tim gave me a big bear hug. I'd missed Tim, the last few days, it had felt like forever since I felt my connection with him. I honestly thought I had lost my friendship with him, he meant more than I even knew myself.

'We should get some rest, could be any day now. Good night Tim,' I smiled and walked back to the others. The room was quiet and Brad was out for watch as we settled in for the night.

'Everyone up now!' we heard Brad shout as we opened our eyes.

Courageous

The cave was in panic with everybody flying everywhere grabbing everything they needed before following Brad's grave orders, Adam was shouting at everyone giving hope and encouraging words. 'Stand up and fight for your kind, do not show them any weakness,' I heard Adam's speech in the background.

'Chloe you're out first, we will be right behind you,' Adam ordered. I took a deep breath ready to face our enemies with my head held high and my weapons by my side. I zipped my jacket up ready for action. Every step I took leaving the cave I grew stronger, with more anger. I felt the adrenaline running through my body, making me shake, not with fear but with ambition to succeed. I made the clearing only to see in my surprise it wasn't Zak on our territory. 'Tate,' I whispered; his creations were close behind him.

'Chloe. Such an honour, to be in your presence today,' Tate spoke in such a way that he seemed rather suspicious.

'Your verdict?' I asked bluntly. He rubbed his chin and started walking over to me, he got so close that his scent became unbearable. I thought I'd be used to it by now with William.

'My verdict, well wouldn't you like to know?' he said walking around me with a smirk. My fists became clenched ready for his attack. 'I must say Chloe; you do rather intrigue me with your attitude and how you do not fear me. You're someone I'd like to have on my team, if you weren't female,' he said, laughing at his own words. 'I'll tell you what pumpkin, we will do a deal. I won't fight you nor against you if you lead the pack, but I will fight with you against those hunters, if your alpha stands down and lets you command in his place.'

I couldn't think of a deal any worse. *Me, lead a fight? I have no experience in combat, besides Adam would never stand down to me if Tate is running the shots.* 'This deal isn't something I can take without alpha permission; you know that Tate. Why would I accept such a deal?' I asked.

'To see how desperate Adam is; and to use your strength, why else would I be here hmm? It's either a deal or death. Which one will it be?' he asked with not a care. I couldn't answer without Adam, *where are they?* I wondered. They'd said they would be right behind me, I turned looking for them. Still no one in sight 'Tick-tock I haven't got all day dear,' he said with sarcasm.

I felt the presence of them getting closer and I smiled with relief, knowing I was no longer on my own with this mad man. Adam was still in his human form, the rest had all phased including William. William stood behind me, not even trying to go back to his own leader like a lap-dog.

'Adam you must stand down and let me lead if we are to fight together with the new ones. If not we must face death, the choice is yours,' I said, loudly for all to hear, bluntly. 'Sorry,' I whispered looking into his eyes.

He nodded back, 'You are worthy to lead, with a true bloodline it is in your nature to be a good alpha. I put mine and the pack's life in your hands,' Adam responded making it all very real. For months all we had thought about was this fight and today we finished it.

'You've got your answer,' I told Tate, with my voice full of spite. I knew I'd be the one communicating but I didn't sign up for temporary alpha. *Their lives are in my hands,* I thought.

'Now what?' I asked Tate. He backed off and put his hands behind his back looking to talk business.

'I've sent men out to set a two-mile perimeter, as soon as they are near they will give us a warning and regular updates through the hand radio devices. We will be ready for them and we will have our positions. Until then we will set up a camp here where we are all together and me and Chloe will set up a fight plan,' Tate informed us.

'No, set up camp away from our territory, it's a risk even you knowing our living quarters.' I now had to spend an evening one to one with Tate, I couldn't imagine a better thing to do in my time of need. Tate stared at me with a blank expression as if I had insulted his battle plans.

He went into his pocket and pulled out the radio and pressed it to speak, 'We are moving location, we are going to the Pitt so move perimeter, same distance in the new location. Over and out.'

The pit? We all looked at each over with confusion. It couldn't be near as we had been miles out hunting in the past. 'Where is the pit, is it far?' I asked with curiosity.

'The Pitt is just further south from here, about half a day on foot or an hour on four legs. But you're alpha I let you decide?' When Tate spoke I sensed a dig at me. I got cross when it came to phasing as I didn't want the others to walk and tire themselves. Yet I don't trust Tate enough for them to be on their own with him. He nodded, sensing my confusion and waiting for my decision.

'On foot, but if I think for one second you're putting us in danger en-route to this destination I will have my pack phase,' I demanded, and crossed my arms.

'Some one scared they will need protecting?' Tate smirked, and the others laughed behind him.

I felt the exact way I felt when I first met William, irritated and wanting to rip someone's head off. He was making my blood boil, just when I thought we could be civil. 'I don't need protecting and I don't need your stupid comments, I may not be able to phase but I could take you on any day!' I said with anger in my voice.

'Well I must say you do have a bite, and maybe I might enjoy you trying to win. Let's just get on with the task at hand hmm?' he said acting superior.

I narrowed my eyes and moved my arm out, ready for him to direct. *So not only do we have to put up with him over night we have to hike with Tate and his pack*. I looked down to William and nodded for them to all dash and phase. One by one they returned fully clothed in a matter of minutes. William was the last to come and came over to meet me.

'Hope you know what you're doing? Tate isn't the sort of person who takes threats and forgets,' William said, looking wary.

'Yeah but I'm not the sort of person who actually cares what sort of person Tate is,' I replied with confidence.

'You should,' William said with such care, William sounded cute with his well-spoken accent, now that I liked him.

'Time to go,' I called out to my pack. I had to admit giving orders did feel more natural than strange, even though I thought Rob was more unhappy than Adam was about my new position.

We moved out from the bottom of the lake, both alphas leading, and both packs separated, and poor William stuck in the middle. The weather was warming up with the odd patch of snow left under the ferns. I could feel the sun beaming down on us in the gaps of the tall trees we walked beneath, a slight breeze flowing through my hair and every now and then the stench from Tate. No-one had said a word since we started our travels. It was nice to have time for my thoughts.

I still pictured Charlie every now and then, I wished to have his arms around me helping me feel that warm feeling I felt so lost without. He kept me safe in a way I had never thought I needed. I hoped he kept his distance for now, if only I had had one more moment with him before we left. It was always in the back of my mind, the thought of my not returning from either death or fear, but as I could not feel I guess it was not a problem. Charlie was my weakness. I was in danger when he was around and I understood this now. I didn't feel excited for the future, only that I still wanted one and didn't want to lose. Sometimes I wondered what it would be like if I just stayed with the pack and settled down, *what else am I supposed to do?*

I came away from my thoughts. We had been walking for some time. The sky was overcast with grey clouds; looking behind me I saw the pack looking bored and miserable. *How long have we got left?* I wondered.

'You'll like the Pitt Chloe it's nice and open and slightly lower with a nice border of grass banks and the odd tree, perfect for getting the hunter off guard, well those who can phase. So has Adam filled you in on the alpha duty of war?' he asked.

Duty of war? It sounds so formal, Adam hadn't said a word to me, only that he hadn't been too disappointed to drop out.

'No, I only know my duty is to lead the pack and they know what they are doing anyway. They're not silly,' I replied with confidence.

'So I guess you know it's down to us to get rid of Zak? I vote you do it and get it over with,' Tate said casually, like killing Zak was no biggie.

'Hang on, you're telling me it's alpha versus leader? Is this why you asked Adam to drop down? So we could be defeated? Is this part of your master plan?' I said, vexed.

Adam touched my shoulder and I looked at him with anger and disappointment. 'Calm down,' he said.

I snapped back, 'I don't take orders from you anymore so back off, I'm in this mess because of you,' I raised my voice to him.

'So that's it?' I snapped back at Tate.

He laughed and stood still, he pointed at me and paused. 'Your bite and feistiness is the plan, that rage inside you I just want to open you like a can of worms and see what you have got. Having Adam as alpha would be like giving Zak a pussy cat to play with, no offence,' he said looking to Adam.

There was giggling in the background from the new breeds. I shook my head and continued walking on.

I got the feeling we were close, the scent I smelled was off. Maybe because I was surrounded by new breeds, but I sensed more ahead.

I looked to Tate in confusion, he looked back just as confused as I was. He rushed off to run up the bank on the side of the track we had been on. He forced the overgrown bushes and ferns out of his way, I followed quickly behind him.

'Chloe wait!' shouted Ben. 'It could be a set up,' he continued. I looked back and then continued to follow Tate.

I saw him frozen ahead at the top of the bank. I climbed up and stood next to him to see two new breeds in the middle of the meadow which I was guessing was the pit. I saw Tate's concentration as he looked at all his boys. His expression turning bitter. I stood in silence working out why Tate stood so still staring at his pack members. From a distance it just looked like they were waiting for us to set up camp. I focused hard to see what Tate could see.

It looked like they had moved, and very still, a noise from Adam's radio crackled. I could not see the boys in the distance holding one. Tate slowly picked the radio out of his pocket, I looked down the bank at the others and put my hand up asking them to stay, and then nodded to my pack, within a flash the pack had phased, I put my hand on my lips to give them a clue. The radio crackled again, he pushed the button and released it, not saying a word.

'Ah so you must be Tate,' a dark voice came from the radio, we looked at each other, looked ahead and saw two men walk from behind the trees in the meadow. 'As you can see we have your guys, but don't worry they did give up a good fight before we got some information,' the voice from the radio continued.

'Let them go,' Tate said, bitter. And in the distance the men untied some rope by the trees and the two boys dropped to the ground. Tate let out a grunt and his left eye twitched. I could see now that the boys were dead, looking at Tate's face was like looking at someone who had just lost something really important. Maybe their pack wasn't so unfamiliar, so different from ours.

'Give me the girl, I'd like to meet my aunt's niece and see for myself if she is so unique,' Zak replied; we could now confirm Zak was here. Tate gave me a shove and I frowned at him in disgust. He wanted to hand me over on a plate to save his own skin.

'Coward,' I whispered to him. Tate narrowed his eyes at me; I really couldn't have cared less if I offended him.

I walked towards him with my head held high taking my time, my heart was racing fast with adrenaline. Moments like this I wished I could phase but I was glad I was not afraid and my emotions were my weakness, without them I was careless. I was getting close to the middle of the opening, by the two gigantic trees where the new breeds' bodies lay limp on the ground. I saw a young man walking towards me, he was moving his neck in a round motion like he was clicking his neck.

His hair was short all over, making it hard to tell his hair colour. His eyes were just a natural grey-blue colour, his skin was lightly tanned. His physique was athletic and he held himself strong as he walked. His scent smelt beautiful, similar to Charlie's, but I didn't feel attracted. His face was pleasant to look at and he had slight stubble. His clothes were baggy, he had a tracksuit and a hoody on. He looked more like a thug than someone intimidating.

'So finally we meet! I've been waiting for this moment for a long time. You're a bit of a late bloomer compared to the others I've come across. But you are most definitely special,' Zak said in a deep calm voice, like we had just bumped into each other at the shops. I knew I was different, but I had never thought I was all that different from the others.

'Special?' I asked.

'Well I hardly ever come across a female true bloodline. Wouldn't want to feel your bite, ouch,' Zak replied.

'That's the least of your worries, my bite,' I replied, confident.

'You see this is why you cannot exist, your existence is a risk to humanity,' Zak said, like I should have agreed.

'I wouldn't hurt humans; it's not in our nature. We protect humans, that's why we exist. Did no one teach you our history?' I asked.

'Yes I know all about your ancestors but it didn't stop you so called legends changing people to your kind. I mean, who wants to become a panther? Or asks to be? No-one! Which means they are made to be,' Zak said, sounding more bitter.

'Humans are not the same, they all have different personalities. Some good people and some evil people. Have you ever heard of a black legend murder people? Except your kind of course,' I said still with confidence.

Zak held his answer back; he rubbed his stubbly chin and looked around. I was still looking directly at his face with my arms by my side. The sun started beaming through the clouds and I looked behind to see more hunters behind him. They looked like ordinary people, of different ethnicities and styles.

'So how's my cousin been? I hear he visited Jane recently. She is still pretty shaken up about the visit,' he said with a grin on his face.

I heard a loud roar behind me and felt breath on my back, I sensed Ben next to me. I turned and put my hand on Ben's back to communicate. He showed me Aunt Jane and her bruises.

'Was it you who hurt Jane? He asks,' I asked for him. Zak frowned in confusion. He looked at Ben and looked at me.

'You shouldn't be able to communicate like that. How?' he questioned me.

'Did you hurt Aunt Jane?' I asked again firmly.

'Yes I did; she was taking to long for information. She's violating the code,' he replied. To which Ben roared and snapped his jaw at him in disgust.

'And what code is this? A code in which you can beat an older woman? Do you not have any respect for family?' I asked, getting angry and annoyed.

'When a legend comes of age or is discovered they must be reported. We checked on you to see if you are or aren't one, we needed to know whether to exterminate vermin. Family isn't family if they have violated the first code, never mate or connect with a female or male legend. So Ben isn't my cousin, he is vermin, just like his father,' Zak said, being bitter.

The hunter's ways are so twisted and cruel. Our ways are a lot more civilised, we wouldn't kill unless it was for food, but never humans or hurt our family.

'Ben's mother, however, is one of you, so technically he is half of you. How does this mean he isn't your family? Are you vermin too?' I asked, sarcastic.

His face began to tense in anger, his hands went into a fist. I could see him change colour to red, like I was making his blood boil. I didn't understand how they came up with codes that did not make sense.

We were made out to be evil, disgusting creatures, if only they knew how we just loved to be in peace and hunt our dinner and play together. We weren't new breeds who changed people just for extra numbers. Though, yes, I knew some of us were changed at a young age.

I still wondered why, and what the story was behind the others, but not one pack member complained about who they were. I used to see a beautiful monster but now I saw we were just beautiful creatures trying to survive in harmony. I could see clearly now; I saw what I was fighting for.

'Vermin! Me vermin? You may be pretty but I'm happy to rearrange your face,' Zak said and spat on the floor in front of me. 'How dare you insult me? You should be begging for your life. How stupid are you?' he asked. *Me beg?* I thought, I laughed, and laughed louder. Him asking me to beg was more funny than a threat.

'I don't think you are in a good position to be laughing when there are only three of you here. Unless the rest of the pack is hiding? Hmm, and why is a new breed in your pack anyway?' he asked in wonder.

I ignored his questions and let out a loud whistle to command the others. I turned my head to face their direction. The sight was marvellous, both packs mixings and coming down the bank. Leading, giants, such strength. I looked back to Zak his face was pale in surprise, we hadn't outnumbered him but the shocking sight of two packs working alongside each other wasn't something you saw every day.

He let out a cough and played with his hands like a nervous twitch. 'Did I forget to mention? We don't have codes. We can mix with which and who ever we like,' I said cockily. I stared directly at him, I was actually starting to get impatient. 'You going to kill me or what? Because this conversation is getting boring,' I said, rolling my eyes.

The hunters were drawing in close behind Zak, they did not look pleased with how confident I was. I put my head to my side and shrugged my shoulders. I turned and winked at the others, they all let out a mighty roar. I noticed Tate was cowering in the background. I turned back and one of the hunters had started running towards me with such aggression. Zak raised his arm and commanded him to stand down.

'She's mine!' he shouted.

Two seconds felt like forever waiting for the move.

I put my foot and my head forward ready, Ben moved in too. The others had lined up, my pack to the left and new breeds to the right. The tension was building up; Zak lowered his hand in one quick motion, staring at me. I ran at Zak at full speed, with one thing on my mind. Defeat.

Zak slid to the floor to kick my legs out, but I power jumped over him and flipped down to land. As I lifted my head up, his leg just missed me as he tried to kick me. He tried again and I grabbed his lower leg, the force of his kick was surprisingly hard, pushing me back. I pushed forward, as hard as I could and sent him back. I threw a fist into his rock-hard abs. For someone who didn't feel pain like humans it still really hurt, but I held it together. He went to hit me and I managed to block his hard punch.

He kicked my chest and sent me flying. I landed on a big branch and felt my back hurt from the force of hitting it. I had no time to think, he was walking over. I ran at full speed and leapt up towards him and grabbed his head in a head lock and flipped him over. The sound of his body hitting the ground gave me pleasure. I twisted myself on top of him and punched his head repeatedly. I could hardly see any damage from letting my rage out on Zak, he tried to block me. He struggled and wiggled, and flipped me under him. He grabbed my hair and hit me. I felt something crack and I could taste blood, he'd struck me again. My head flew back. My body struggled to cope with the blow of his punches.

I heard a faint roar in the distance, and out of nowhere I saw Tim leap and push Zak off me. I turned my head to see Zak wipe blood off his face. Tim was in the pouncing position, ready to attack. He leapt high, with his sharp claws and teeth bared, eyes hungry in revenge. Zak grabbed Tim's ribs as Zak was forced to the ground, Tim still trying to bite Zak. Within a flash I saw Zak crush Tim's ribs. Tim let out a huge wince.

And then I felt it, like an out of body experience. The butterflies and the passion, the memory like a flash back episode exploding in my head. I could feel the bruises heal, energy enter my body like a drug. Heart racing and limbs stiffening. The strange emotions I once was familiar with were back! I sat up and saw Zak looking down at Tim, dusting of his clothes and looking pleased with himself.

Without any thought, I lunged myself at Zak. I felt burning in my muscles and sharp pain as I felt my body wanting to phase. I didn't hold back. I pounced and within a flash I was a beautiful creature, I felt whole again with the pack. I sensed some were injured but I couldn't think of anything else other than finishing Zak. I knocked him down and scratched down his face, he screamed in pain. I roared in his face. Both claws were slightly in his chest.

'What are you waiting for?' he shouted with his face next to my head. So close, but my emotions were changing the way I felt. *Can I actually kill!?* I asked myself as I looked into his eyes.

'Chloe watch out!' I heard a voice shout, I looked over, and to my surprise it was Charlie. I roared in Zak's face, felt a scratch and pulled back. Little did I know Zak had my knife, which must have fallen from my sheath as I phased. He stood, pointing the knife at me. Still stunned, Charlie was on the battlefield, walking between me and Zak.

'I can't let you hurt her,' Charlie said to Zak.

'Are you for real? She's the enemy, please don't tell me you have fallen for her?' Zak asked Charlie in disbelief.

'Yes I have, I've broken one code but if you kill her you would also have broken a code today as well,' Charlie replied. I swallowed hard and felt tense, *how many codes do they actually have, these hunters? I wish I had my voice to tell him to go while he has the chance.*

'Cannot hurt or kill a hunter mate unless they pose a threat,' Charlie strongly pointed out.

'Yes but she's a black legend and she is a threat, look how dangerous Chloe is. If I didn't have a knife in my hand my head would be off my shoulders right now,' Zak replied, cross.

He dropped the knife and put his hand up.

'Stop!' he shouted.

I gasped in horror, bodies were on the ground and injured. I couldn't tell which side was worse off.

I ran over to Tim and nudged him with my head, he groaned. I rested my head on his. He showed me his thoughts and what I saw was beautiful. A picturesque view of the forest, peaceful and butterflies fluttering, all different colours. I saw my face smiling, then I saw Tim embracing me and stroking my hair. He was speaking, telling me everything would be okay and kissing my forehead. His thoughts went blank and I lifted my head. *Tim is gone? No, he can't be*, I thought. I let out a loud distressed roar, with a lump in my throat and dry tears. I felt pain and hurt, I turned to seek revenge.

He's gone? I thought. I started running around trying to find Zak but all the hunters had snuck off leaving just us and Charlie. Within seconds I was back to myself, completely naked but I didn't care. I went back over to Tim's lifeless body. I felt tears roll down my face.

'Why him?' I screamed, 'He was trying to protect me, it should be me!' I sobbed, I was distraught.

I felt a hand on my shoulder, I grabbed the warm hand and looked to see Ben looking hurt and weak.

'The new breeds have disappeared, they took their injured,' he said softly.

'We need to go,' he said, looking at Charlie.

I couldn't feel my legs, I was so weak with grief.

'We can't leave him here! He needs to go where the butterflies flutter and the sun beams and it's peaceful,' I said, struggling to talk.

Ben held out his hand to pick me up and Charlie brought over my clothes that weren't damaged, which only left a long top and jacket I must have taken off without realising. Ben put his arms around me; I looked and nodded at Charlie. He nodded back and walked in their opposite direction.

Promises

We searched for hours to find the perfect burial site, I hadn't said a word since we left. I couldn't even look back to see Brad and Rob carry Tim's body. I felt guilty and disgusting, going over and over in my head. *It's all my fault, they wanted me,* I kept thinking. I looked up in the distance and saw a lovely spot similar to Tim's vision, the sun hit a tree perfectly and a few butterflies fluttered.

'Here. He would like to be here,' I said to Adam.

Adam didn't look at me, he just pointed to a spot by a boulder. William walked next to me and held my hand and smiled.

'It's beautiful here, peaceful,' he said. I squeezed his hand in recognition of his kind words. Brad phased and began to dig a grave, but I couldn't watch. I felt a tear fall down my face.

'So nice to meet you Chloe, know it's bad timing but I'm gathering you're whole again,' he said, trying to make conversation to distract me.

'I'm whole but just feel broken,' words struggled to leave my lips.

It took a while to bury Tim, we all picked wild flowers and placed them on top of the grave. No one said a word but just looked down, looking hurt. William stayed back to give the pack a moment.

'You will be missed buddy,' Brad said, wiping his eyes and stepping back.

'The pack won't be the same without you,' Rob said, and placed one last flower. He followed Brad. Adam and Ben made their peace and walked off and I was left by his side one last time.

'I hope you are now at peace in a place where you can chase the butterflies or have snow ball fights. One day we will be together again, thank you for keeping me safe and welcoming me into your life. You are the kindest, most caring being I know. I will never ever forget you, and how brave you are. I miss you already,' I just couldn't say another word as I broke down and knelt by his side.

'Zak,' I whispered. I stood up to walk off.

'Wait!' Ben shouted, and the others followed.

I turned around, 'I'm going to get him,' I said.

'Get who?' Brad asked.

'I'm going to get Zak to pay, these hunters can't get away with this,' I said, determinedly.

'Well that didn't stop you hanging around with one behind our back,' Adam snapped.

I'd been waiting for Adam to say something about Charlie.

'Charlie saved us, ok? I know it's not ideal and I didn't know who he was when I met him. It still didn't give me the right to continue, but let's not make this about him. Zak is the enemy,' I said.

'The pack is done, we lost our brother today! And you want to seek revenge and he is not even cold yet, I'm sorry but I have no choice but to ask you to leave the pack and come back when you have matured,' Adam said without hesitation.

'You can't do that; I need you all! You want to push me out when I need you all the most,' I pleaded.

'Go!' Adam snapped.

'Fine, but I'm not coming back 'til Zak is gone and then I'll finally be at peace,' I looked to the ground hoping someone would back me up. But no-one spoke for me.

'Bye Brad, Rob, William. Coming with me Ben?' I asked.

He looked at me, showing me remorse.

'Sorry Chloe,' he whispered.

I cannot believe I'm being cast out at a time like this. Not even William is coming to back me. I rubbed my forehead and gave them all one last look, and walked to the north. *I will find Zak and I will finish him.*

The pain in my chest and the anxiety of grief was agonising, I'd been walking and stewing in my guilt. Alone in the wild with no plan or idea where I was going. The forest was getting dark and the moon was full. A sweet aroma filled my nose.

'Charlie!' I cried.

He walked out from the trees in the distance, I ran as fast as I could to hold him tightly. I was probably crushing him; he gently stroked my long hair.

'I'm here,' he said. I looked up and pressed my lips to his, and stroked his hair. A tear rolled down my cheek, he wiped it away.

'I need to get Zak and make him pay, I'm not going to give up and let Tim die in vain,' I said, and looked into Charlie's eyes

'I know, but there is something important you need to know,' Charlie said.

He looked very suspicious and stroked my hair, I sensed negativity.

'Your father is still alive and he is in England, I'd been tracking him down for a while before I met you; he is on the run from the hunters back in the UK. They are tracking down all the true bloodlines starting in England and your father is next on the list.'

I gasped, my father was like me! I felt some closure, but what now? Go and help my long-lost father or get Zak? Today had been more than eventful.

'Let's go,' I said as Charlie grabbed my hand.

'Where are we heading on our new adventure?' he asked.

I paused as I made my decision.

'England.'